ALIENS ABDUCTED MY HEART

AWAKENED WOMB BOOK 1

HAWKE OAKLEY

You'll receive an exclusive short story by signing up for my newsletter! You will also be the first to know about new releases, sales, and illustrated art of my boys.

Sign Up Here

or go to www.hawkeoakley.com

HAWKE OAKLEY

It occurred to me twenty minutes before our crash landing that the blinking red light above the console was probably a bad thing.

But the Levi from twenty minutes ago wasn't concerned with that. What *did* concern him was that he had to appear calm, cool, and collected to the other two men on board the ship. Because that's what captains did. Captains weren't supposed to botch their first big interstellar mission because they were afraid of looking stupid.

Unfortunately, crashing your spaceship on an alien planet very much constitutes stupidity. Good job, Captain Levi.

Before all hell broke loose, I was sitting in the cockpit double-checking the coordinates to our destination. Despite all the advances in technology, teleportation was still out of reach, so it would be a few hours before we reached the designated planet. My team was part of an ongoing correspondence with their leaders. Our job was to make first contact. We'd ensure their planet hadn't blown up, and that they weren't trying to make *our* planet blow up.

It was a simple job. That's why they only sent three men on the ship. Me, the captain; one diplomat; and one doctor, just in case. The ship was relatively small, and most of the upkeep was automated, including food preparation and landing protocols. In theory, all I had to do was steer.

Easy, right?

Haha, *no*.

"Hey, Levi?" Paz asked.

Great. Not only was the blinking red light situation happening, but someone else was here to witness it. I put on a confident smile that I hoped didn't look too forced and straightened my shoulders.

"Yes, Paz?" I said.

He gestured casually above the console. "That light's been blinking for a while now."

Paz was our diplomat, and since his name meant 'peace,' I could only assume his parents had wanted that to be his future career.

"Yes, it has," I replied. My smile didn't fade as I scrolled through some flight information on a separate screen in an attempt to look like I was doing something important.

Paz tilted his head. "It's not, like, a problem, right?"

His tone implied that he was trying his hardest not to offend me while hoping to sate his morbid curiosity.

"Oh no, not at all," I said, giving him a smile.

God, I hoped I didn't just lie to him.

My response made his shoulders slacken. "Okay, *capitão*. Just checking." To my horror, he sat down in the spare seat next to me and riffled through his pack before pulling out a stick of gum. "Want one?"

"No, thanks."

He shrugged and tossed a piece in his mouth. The overwhelming scent of artificial cherry was a momentary distraction from the stupid light.

"How far away is this planet again?" Paz asked.

"A couple hours."

Blink. Blink. Blink.

A bead of sweat rolled down my brow. I ignored it.

Paz yawned and stretched, nearly knocking his arm into me. "You'd think engineers could design faster ships by now, huh?"

I grunted in response. My stiff hands kept rooting through the information trees on the screen. I was trying to find out the light's purpose as discreetly as possible. At least Paz seemed more interested in reading the joke on the back of his gum wrapper than in what I was doing.

"Hey, Levi—"

"You know, it's Captain Levi," I said before punching the troubleshooting menu.

"Right. Hey, what do you call a male alien who's interested in another male?"

The troubleshooting menu had no mention of the blinking light. I ground my teeth and broadened my search terms.

"Do you know what the answer is?" Paz asked, grinning. "A *gaylien*! Man, that one's cheesy…"

I sure wished a gaylien mechanic would come fix this fucking light right now.

"How about this one—"

Paz was interrupted by a loud, neutral-toned beep.

My blood ran cold.

"What was that?" Paz asked mid-chew.

"Nothing," I said quickly.

This wasn't my first time piloting a ship. I was a

seasoned captain with thousands of hours of practice flights and real low-orbit ones. Never in that time had I seen this irritating red light, or heard that godforsaken ominous tone.

And then the worst possible thing happened: the blinking light and the tone synced up.

They were related to each other.

A string of curses ran through my head. The tone was an alarm, one that went hand-in-hand with the visual light cue. That could only mean that whatever malfunction the light indicated was getting worse. More urgent.

"Guess that's not your choice of in-flight playlist?" Paz asked.

"Don't worry about it. Everything's under control," I said through my teeth. It had to be. Otherwise...

Actually, I didn't want to think about otherwise.

Now I was starting to freak out. I checked the map system. Our destination was light-miles away. There was no way we'd reach it before whatever was wrong with the ship struck first.

I had to stay calm. I didn't know for a fact what was wrong, so there was no need to jump to conclusions. Maybe it was just alerting me to the lack of ice in the juice machine.

The tone got louder.

Okay, fine. It wasn't the juice machine.

"This track would sound better with vocals," Paz joked.

At least he was still in a good mood. Meanwhile I was rapidly descending into panic. Not a good look for a captain.

Stay calm, I repeated. *The others need you to focus.*

As if on cue, the sliding door opened behind me.

"What is that racket?" Jaeyoung grumbled.

Paz grinned. "It's Levi's hot new track, available on starTunes."

"Hilarious," Jaeyoung deadpanned.

I chewed the inside of my cheek. Jaeyoung was a doctor, but he also had a degree in engineering. If I swallowed my pride, I could ask him for help. But this was *my* mission, the first serious one I'd ever been sent on. Asking for help would make me sound weak, or worse, incompetent. I couldn't let the admiral think I was some newbie who didn't know what he was doing. I deserved this position as much as any of the older pilots, and I'd prove it.

Was the light getting redder or was it just my frayed nerves?

I felt the gazes of both my crewmates boring into my head. They trusted me. I couldn't let them down.

This ship was *not* crashing, dammit.

...But just in case it did, I swiped the map closer to our coordinates. My heart flipped when I saw a nearby planet, one we could reach within minutes if needed. We were flying right over it and I hadn't even noticed. How was that possible?

I furrowed my brow at this odd new planet. There shouldn't have been a planet here at all, not according to my maps, positioning systems, and general knowledge. It was like the planet only appeared to the naked eye after the ship's automated systems failed... Did it have some kind of masking presence to avoid detection?

"That's not our destination," Jaeyoung said behind me.

My jaw tightened. Unlike Paz, he didn't miss anything. My pride wanted to tell him to stop backseat piloting, even though I secretly wanted his help.

"We might need to stop here and refuel," I said, hoping my lie wasn't paper-thin.

But if my lie was paper, Jaeyoung was a pair of scissors. "We have more than enough fuel for the entire round trip. What's going on, Levi?"

My gut twisted. I wasn't even annoyed that he didn't call me "captain"—I certainly didn't feel like one right now. Not a good one, anyway.

Just as I debated whether to keep lying or fess up, the whole cockpit was bathed in red.

My heart dropped like a stone. Now the whole ship screamed, 'hey, asshole, something's broken!'

Paz glanced at me, looking nervous. "That's not mood lighting, is it?"

"No," I admitted.

Upon hearing the note of dread in my voice, Jaeyoung charged closer to the console, gripping my shoulder hard as he leaned in to see it.

"Shit, Levi," he muttered. "Why didn't you tell me sooner?"

My ears flushed hot with shame. He was right, but admitting it felt like walking on coals.

"Wait, what?" Paz asked, his voice going up an octave.

Unfortunately, I could no longer reassure him. I was just as baffled as he was.

Jaeyoung scowled at me, his face menacing in the red glow of the cockpit. He had to raise his voice over the alarm's increased volume. "Tell me what's happening. Are we going down?" he demanded.

I grimaced. "I don't know."

Jaeyoung didn't waste time scolding me. His fingers flew over the screen, but all he did was cycle through the same useless menus that I did.

"Are we seriously gonna crash?" Paz cried. "Oh my god,

I knew it, I knew I hated space! I don't know why I ever agreed to do this interplanetary diplomacy crap!"

The ship jolted, knocking us sideways. Paz shrieked as my shoulder jarred into him. Jaeyoung cursed under his breath, grabbing the console so he didn't fall.

This was bad. I needed to rein in the situation *now*.

"We won't crash," I stated. I righted myself and grasped the manual controls. "We're going to make an emergency landing."

"Oh, like there's a difference," Paz snarked.

"There is. We might lose the ship, but we'll survive."

"And where exactly is our landing strip? In a black hole?"

"No." I rerouted the map so my crewmates could see the planet below us—the one we were rapidly approaching. "This one."

Jaeyoung frowned. "I don't recognize that planet."

Paz groaned, sinking back in his seat. "Oh, great. Not even the smart guy knows where we are."

The ship sputtered, violently shaking the interior. I gripped the controls harder and forced them steady. The ship shuddered and stalled, then I felt the explosion of energy against its hull when we entered the planet's airspace. Paz was thrown out of his seat. He yelped as he tumbled across the floor. Jaeyoung grunted with effort as he gripped a bolted-down chair for dear life.

The strange new planet approached fast. I only saw it as a blur of color: pink, green, and blue, all tainted by the blaring red of the cockpit. The ship shook so hard I couldn't make out any discernible features of the terrain. I desperately hoped we would land on something soft.

"Everybody hold on!" I yelled.

The ship entered a freefall; the controls were no longer responsive. I yanked the manual controls, steering the ship as best I could as we plummeted towards the foreign ground.

Gay or not, I just prayed the aliens here weren't hostile.

A FOUL-SMELLING plume rose from the Sweetfields. The billowing black cloud could only be one thing: smoke.

The acrid scent soured my mood. I was in the middle of gathering herbs, but that would have to wait. I tossed my basket down and sprang into a gallop on all fours—running was much faster on multiple limbs. My long front arms and powerful back legs swallowed up the ground, propelling me towards the source of the smoke.

Fire was the ultimate enemy. It never occurred naturally on Eukaria.

Was it arson? To harm the Sweetfields, our brethren and one of our greatest treasures, was punishable by death. Whoever harmed the plants and creatures there would pay.

I raced over the expanse of rugged moss until the Sweetfields came into view. Their iconic colorful stalks were taller than the largest Maeleon. But a hard lump formed around my heart when I saw the foul blaze with my own eyes.

Who dared do such a horrible thing? What kind of heathen would set innocent plants ablaze?

Fury spurred me onward. It wasn't until I saw the sterile

silver mass lying oblong in the field that I realized something was horribly wrong.

I stalled, my body freezing. Light gleamed off its too-smooth sides, and smoke spewed from its vents. The sight of the unnatural thing gave me chills.

Could it be...?

I'd heard stories of space-faring ships before, but I thought they were myths. Legends. Beings from other planets who entered metal deathtraps to explore, or worse, conquer. It sounded like an elaborate tale for entertainment. But my assumptions were wrong. The flaming hull in front of me was real.

As I got closer, the ship's black smoke petered out into hot steam. I hoped there was no more fuel to burn and the craft's dying breaths came soon.

I looked around. Among the wreckage, I saw nobody. Perhaps if there had been creatures inside, they had already perished.

But then I heard a voice, one too soft and wispy to belong to a Maeleon. Those sounds couldn't come from a hard, scaly maw.

The voice originated from the other side of the ship. I used the crashed heap to my advantage. I kept close to the hull, inwardly sneering at its ugliness, and stalked around the side. Heat still radiated off the metal, hurting the plants beneath it.

"I'm sorry, little siblings," I murmured. It was too late to save them, but I'd stop the beings from harming any more of our kin.

Two more distinct voices spoke up. Were there three in total?

I was too far away to hear distinct words—and even if I did, I doubted I could understand their language—but I inferred the gist of their conversation from their tone. The first voice appeared to belong to their leader. He spoke in a confident, reassuring way. There was a quality about it that intrigued me.

I angled my ear to hear the other two. One was higher pitched, squawking with fear. The second was deeper, irritated.

We were not a violent species, but if these beings came to Eukaria only to destroy, they would be dealt with accordingly.

My heart picked up speed. What kind of beings would I find on the other side? My feelers tingled, picking up minute vibrations in the air. I sensed frayed nerves and unease from the newcomers.

No longer able to contain my curiosity, I stepped out to face them.

They were... unusual.

The first thing I noticed was their short height. They stood upright on two legs, the same as Maeleons, but the similarities ended there. Strange identical coverings swallowed their bodies so only their heads were exposed. They lacked horns, tails, tentacles, and manes of feelers. Their ears were tiny rounded shells, their faces oddly blunt. Their soft flesh resembled the delicate surface of a newly bloomed petal.

They were small, frail-looking things. Where were their scales? Their bright, flashy colors?

I examined them closer. The three creatures had different facial features, heights, and flesh and fur colors, yet were clearly all the same species.

I sniffed the air. Except for the sweaty tang of fear, the beings smelled oddly sterile. I wondered if the scent of the unnatural silver ship rubbed off on them. How long had they been in there? Did they live in those things? There was so much I did not know.

I wanted to examine the newcomers longer, but the shortest creature—the one with light brown skin—shrieked. It fell backwards, staring at me wide-eyed, thrusting a shaky finger in my direction.

"N-n-n-newcomer!" it cried.

Newcomer? That wasn't right. This planet was my homeland—these beings were the newcomers, not me.

But how did I understand its words? We couldn't have spoken the same language.

Since communication was an option, I replied, "That is not correct."

The other two creatures jolted and stared at me. The tallest one had pitch-dark hair and discerning eyes. It looked calmer than the panicking one on the ground.

But the third newcomer...

As I focused on him, my feelers went rigid.

Its skin was pale pink and looked soft to the touch. A tuft of dusty yellow fur sat on its head, and its eyes—

My feelers shivered. Its eyes were a cool jade green, the same as my scales.

What an absolutely beautiful creature.

"It talked," the green-eyed one murmured. The sound made my spine tingle. Even its voice was perfect.

"Yes." I gestured with my tail to the creature on the ground. "So did that one. How did it do that?"

The ground-dweller sounded flustered. "My name is Paz. And I'm a *he*, not an *it*."

"*He*?" I responded, testing out the strange sound on my tongue. "What does this mean?"

The three creatures exchanged glances, as if confused.

"Jaeyoung, try speaking without the interstellar transla-tion module," Green-Eyes suggested.

The tall one with black fur on its head tapped its ear. I noticed the newcomers all shared a curved, silver apparatus on a single ear. I had assumed it was part of their bodies, but the tall one removed it and began to speak. This time, a garbled mess of sounds emerged.

Green-Eyes tilted its head and asked, "Did you under-stand that?"

"No," I said.

The tall one—Jaeyoung—replaced the silver ear device. "That explains it. Good to know our ITMs are functional."

"What is *he*?" I asked again, not comprehending that word.

Green-Eyes explained, "It's a pronoun. The one we all use. So, the three of us are *he*, not *it*. Does that make sense?"

"No," I admitted. "But I will try to remember."

Paz stood up and dusted off his coverings. "These newcomers must have different gender customs."

"I am not a newcomer," I interjected. "You three are the newcomers."

Jaeyoung nodded. "I see. The connotation of the word —" He removed his device and said something like *ay-lee-un* before replacing it. "—must be different in their language. So, it translates as 'newcomer.' Compared to the word *he*, which does not exist at all."

I stared at Green-Eyes throughout the explanation. He had long hairs that framed his eyelids. They reflected sunlight, making them glow. I did not yet know this stunning creature's name. I was more interested in that than his cultural exchange.

"What are you called?" I demanded.

Green-Eyes stood up straighter, meeting my gaze firmly.

"My name is Levi. I'm the captain of this ship." At once, his eyes widened as he remembered something important. He jerked towards the smoking spacecraft. "Dammit, the ship!"

Levi rushed to the silver hull. He groaned, miserably running his small hands down its sides. Was it important to him? I didn't care for the unnatural thing, but I did not like seeing him upset.

"What is wrong?" I asked, stepping closer to him.

From the corner of my eye, I noticed Jaeyoung and Paz watching me closely. If they were Maeleons, they would've noticed from my relaxed body language that I meant him no harm. But they were not, so I had to use my words. I was grateful their devices allowed us to communicate with ease.

"It's all right. I would never hurt him," I told them, hoping it would assuage their concern.

Levi's cheek pressed against the hull as he sighed. "The ship is totally wrecked. All because of that damned light…"

"The red light that kept beeping?" Paz asked, his voice sharp with irritation. "You said it was nothing! Why didn't you tell us? Now we're stuck on this weird planet!"

When Levi winced, my stomach knotted in sympathy. I didn't want them to argue, and I didn't want Levi's feelings to be hurt.

But I recalled one important fact. Their ship's wreckage harmed the Sweetfields, whether intentional or not. It was my duty to report to the other villagers.

"I must tell the others what happened here," I said solemnly.

Paz's eyes widened. "There are more of you?"

"You know, Paz, for a diplomat, you could stand to be more thoughtful with your language," Jaeyoung noted in a neutral tone. "We're on a different planet talking to a sentient, speaking being. It makes sense it would be a social creature."

Paz ducked his head. "Yeah, you're right."

Levi regarded me, his gorgeous green eyes searching my face. "What's your name?"

He was interested in me, too. I was happy.

"I am called Zat'tor," I replied.

Levi nodded, then took a deep breath, as if preparing himself for an unpleasant experience. "All right. Zat'tor, please take us to your leader."

Paz groaned. "Did you seriously just use that reference?"

"I wasn't trying to make a reference," Levi grumbled.

The term confused me. What did he mean by that?

"I am the leader," I told him.

Levi stood up straighter, like I'd suddenly gained importance. "Y-you are?"

"Yes. Everyone in the village is a leader of alternating tasks," I explained.

"So, there's no, like... *president*? *Prime minister*? *Chieftain*?" Paz asked.

"I do not comprehend," I said, baffled by his strange words.

"No strict hierarchical system. Fascinating," Jaeyoung murmured, poking his thin fingers against a screen on his wrist.

Levi cleared his throat, squaring his shoulders. Even at his most upright posture, he was a head shorter than me. He was so adorably tiny that I wanted to wrap my feelers around him like a carnivorous plant swallowing an insectoid whole.

How odd. I'd never experienced such an urge before.

"Allow me to explain, Zat'tor," Levi said. "I'm the

captain of this crew, which makes me the leader. My crew takes orders from me. But it also means their lives are my responsibility. So, for the sake of my crew and my mission, please help us return home."

He performed a strange gesture. He bent his upper body forward at the waist, keeping his arms at his sides while lowering his head to me. He resembled a wilting flower. Was he sick? Worried, I put my claws on his shoulders and eased him back upright.

A bright pink color erupted across Levi's cheeks. That surprised me. I didn't know he could change colors.

"W-what are you doing?" Levi asked.

"You looked unwell," I explained.

Levi blinked his wide green eyes. They shone bright above the pink bloom on his cheeks. "Oh, um, thank you. I'm fine. I was bowing. I guess it's a human thing."

"Human," I repeated slowly. "Is that what you are?"

He nodded. "Yes. What are you, Zat'tor?"

"I am a Maeleon. My kind lives on this beautiful world we call Eukaria."

"Eukaria," Jaeyoung mused, still poking his device. "Almost like the English word eukaryote."

"Well, it's nice to meet you," Levi said. He sounded honest, but there was a wariness in his tone. "I can't say I've met a Maeleon before, or even heard of them."

"Then I am glad to be the first," I said.

Levi held out his small, pink hand expectantly. Was this like 'bowing'?

Eager to meet him halfway, I extended my tentacles. Levi yelped in surprise as my second pair of limbs floated towards him. I placed the tips of my suction-cup pads around his hand. The inner side was softer and squishier than the outside.

As I gripped Levi's hand, I felt him shiver. The pink color on his cheeks flared deeper.

"Ah," he said lightly. "I didn't realize you had... tentacles."

"And you do not," I noted.

How did humans do anything without tentacles? Or feelers? What a strange species.

Levi slowly pulled his hand back. "You can, er, let go now. Human handshakes usually only last a few seconds."

That was what he said, but he didn't sound entirely confident. Nevertheless, I released his doughy little appendage. I was a bit saddened by its loss.

"Hey, Zat'tor?" Paz asked, pointing at the shipwreck. "You said you needed to tell 'the others' what happened here. Does that mean we're in trouble?"

"Yes," I said. "Very much so."

All three humans' face's blanched.

"What kind of trouble?" Paz asked.

I flicked my tail towards the charred plants beneath the ship. "Setting the Sweetfields ablaze is our ultimate taboo. It is rare that a Maeleon would ever commit such a crime, but the punishment ranges from exile to sacrifice."

"Sacrifice?" Paz squeaked.

"Yes. In exchange for the lost lives of plants, the perpetrator is killed in honor of the Soul of Eukaria, so their corpse may dissolve into fertilizer to feed new germinations."

Paz whimpered as his knees buckled. Levi caught him, hauling the other human to his feet to keep him from collapsing. Then he thrust Paz's half-limp body at Jaeyoung and stepped towards me.

"Wait, Zat'tor," Levi said urgently. The rosy hue was gone from his cheeks. Now they were as pale as a withered leaf. "The crash landing was an accident. We meant no harm to you, or your plants. Let's work something out, okay?"

His offer intrigued me. I had no intention of letting anything bad happen to Levi—I still wanted to wrap my feelers around his little body and keep him to myself forever. But it boded well for our future that he was willing to help resolve this conflict.

"Yes. We shall work out a solution. This pleases me," I said. To help guide Levi, I laid a tentacle across his shoulders. It made his cheeks change color again. "Come with me. Let us discuss your judgment, humans."

Great. First I crash landed on a foreign planet and fucked up my very first mission, and now my whole crew was about to get executed for plant crimes.

Could this day get any worse?

I tried to keep calm as Zat'tor's tentacle rested on my shoulders, like a noose hovering above my neck. Not that he gripped me particularly roughly, but I knew this couldn't end well. *Nothing* involving tentacles ever ended well.

Zat'tor wasn't really a "he," either. The concept of gender seemed—well, alien to him. But since he was tall and muscular, I couldn't help but think of him as male.

As the huge teal alien led us towards his village, I stole nervous glances up at him. He was so... alien-looking. I'd never seen anything like him before. His long mouth was shaped like one of a lizard, or a dragon. He had horns jutting out the back of his head, and a strange mane like a lion—except instead of hair, it was made up of hundreds of long, seaweed-like tendrils that pulsated with subtly changing colors.

During my pilot training, we'd learned all about the

different documented alien species, but Maeleons were new to me. We didn't know about Eukaria or the beings that lived on it, yet somehow our ITMs' translation feature still functioned. I'd wonder why, but I was busy with other pertinent problems.

God, what a clusterfuck this was. I was about to be hanged by the *one* species I knew nothing about. He'd probably do it with his creepy tentacles, too.

But I had to admit, the tentacles were softer than I imagined. They were smooth and dry, not slimy like squid or octopus back on Earth, almost like a snake without scales. Unlike a snake, Zat'tor's tentacles were strangely warm. It would've been comforting if he wasn't leading me to my death.

I was such an idiot. How could I have fucked up this badly? I was supposed to guide my crew to peace and prosperity. I was supposed to keep them safe. Instead, I got fatally distracted by a stupid red blinking light, and now we were about to get turned into plant food.

Think, Levi. There has to be a way out of this mess.

My captain's training activated. Only by keeping calm and thinking it through could we escape. My mind leapt to the worst-case scenario—being sacrificed to the plant overlords—and worked backwards. What was slightly better than execution? Slavery?

I peeked at Zat'tor and gulped. He wasn't ugly by any stretch of the imagination. If anything, his nonhuman features captivated me. If a giant chameleon, an orchid, and the sexiest man alive were thrown into a blender, Zat'tor would be the result. He was huge, effortlessly muscular, and tall. Intelligence shone in his sunset-orange eyes. He was nothing like the aliens I'd learned about in pilot training, or the ugly gray ones in Old Earth works of fiction. The longer I looked at him, the more he enchanted me.

Maybe I could pay my dues in sexual favors or some-thing. That wouldn't be so bad...

I yanked my gaze away. What was I thinking? My alien captor was minutes away from pulverizing me into nutrient soup, and here I was thirsting over him.

Still, I couldn't stop risking peeks at Zat'tor. Call it pilot's curiosity. I always wanted to know more about the world around me—or in this case, the tentacles around me.

Zat'tor caught my gaze.

Shit. Busted.

He had a snout covered in scaly ridges, almost like in Old Earth depictions of dragons, but Zat'tor was no fantas-tical beast. He was real flesh and blood. Strangely, despite the snout, he was able to form human-like expressions.

As Zat'tor held eye contact with me, he seemed to smile. He didn't have lips the same way I did, but he parted his jaws, flashing sharp white teeth in what was definitely a grin.

A shiver rolled down my spine. I couldn't tell if I was scared or horny. Probably both. If I had a private moment with Jaeyoung, he'd probably explain how those two sensa-tions were connected. Not that I wanted to discuss my sex life with my fellow captive crewmate.

Levi, can you please get your mind out of the gutter? Your life is in danger, my brain reminded me.

Right. Escaping the hostile alien planet.

A thought suddenly hit me. Since arriving on Eukaria, we hadn't seen a single other non-plant life form. The only two kinds seemed to be us humans, and the Maeleons. So then, why did Zat'tor have sharp teeth? Surely herbivores didn't need fangs?

Unless... this was all a big trick, and he was leading my crew to his den to devour us all.

Out of nowhere, Zat'tor stopped walking. He angled his head curiously down at me. "What is wrong, Levi?"

"Huh?"

"You feel cold and tense. Do you need warmth?"

I *was* cold and tense. I'd been shivering for the past five minutes. Since, you know, thinking about getting eaten by a giant predator did that to a human's base instincts.

"How do you know that?" I asked, shocked at his perception.

Zat'tor's tentacle squirmed on my shoulders. I jolted. The warm weight of it was so comfortable, I'd forgotten it was there.

Oh, great. I was already being lulled into a false sense of security by the predator.

"My tentacles are sensitive to vibrations and changes in temperature, among other things," Zat'tor explained. "I did not realize humans are ectothermic. If you are cold, I will warm you."

I blinked. "Ecto...?"

"In layman's terms, ectothermic means cold-blooded, like reptiles," Jaeyoung explained behind me.

Part of me wondered why my crewmates were still here. They weren't tied up or bound in any way, not even by one of Zat'tor's tentacles like me. They could've easily run away, but I supposed there was nowhere for them to go. Either that or they *really* wanted to become plant food with me.

Zat'tor leaned in, his scaly brow furrowed in concern. His tentacle tightened around my shoulder. "Come closer to my chest," he urged. "I do not want you to freeze."

My cheeks burned as the wriggly limb squeezed around

me. It kind of felt like getting a massage, but that wasn't the point. I didn't *want* to hug Zat'tor. I think.

"W-wait, there's been a misunderstanding," I said, holding up my hands. "I'm not cold. And I'm not ectothermic. I'm warm-blooded."

"Then why do you shiver?" he asked. As he spoke, I saw the glint of his sharp teeth again.

I sighed. Now I had to give an alien a physiology lesson. This should've been the doctor's job, not mine.

"Humans shiver when they're cold, but also when they're... anxious," I admitted.

Zat'tor sounded startled. "You are anxious? Why?"

There was no use dancing around the point.

"Aren't you going to eat me?" I blurted out. "As in, consume, devour? Use my flesh as food?"

Zat'tor laughed. At least, he made a sound that *seemed* like a human laugh. For all I knew, it might've been a cry of rage in the Maeleon language.

Suddenly, I felt the fleshy 'hand' of Zat'tor's tentacle on top of my head. He patted me like a dog.

"No, Levi," Zat'tor said as if I'd been silly. He continued walking with me in tow. "Why do you think that?"

I coughed as his tentacle ruffled my hair. "Well, your teeth are sharp. On our home planet, fangs usually indicate a creature eats flesh."

Zat'tor inclined his head curiously, like he'd never heard of the concept. "Maeleons use our fangs for eating fruit, and for vigorous intercourse."

Paz choked behind us. Meanwhile, my jaw dropped. That was not the answer I expected.

Trying to keep my composure, I asked, "So, you... *do* have intercourse."

Zat'tor brightened. "Yes. Plenty of it, with the right partner, or partners."

Partners? I thought. For some reason, I got stuck on that word. I was never into sharing, and I didn't like imagining Zat'tor doing it either. Not that it was any of my goddamn business what an alien did with other aliens.

"Ah. For procreation or fun?" I asked.

"Both," Zat'tor replied cheerily. The sex discussion certainly put a pep in his step. Was he imagining it right now?

And if he was, with *who?*

I stomped down the emerging worm of jealousy. What the hell did I have to be jealous about? Zat'tor wasn't my boyfriend—he was an alien leading me to my death.

"We have arrived," Zat'tor announced.

I'd been so preoccupied with the sex talk that I hadn't noticed the village in front of us. My eyes widened in awe. It was straight out of a children's fairy tale. Each dwelling unit was made of vines thicker than a steel beam, twisting together like woven rattan furniture. A pond stood at the center of the village, sparkling in the sunlight.

It hadn't occurred to me until now that Eukaria was full of water. It had to be to support all the plant life.

"Whoa," Paz murmured. "There's more Maeleons."

My two crewmates took in the scene with amazement, acting more like tourists than captives. Although technically, *they* weren't being held captive. Only I had Zat'tor's tentacle wrapped firmly around my shoulders like a long, soft, possessive pillow.

Just as Paz said, other Maeleons strolled around the village. They all seemed to be going about their day like usual until they noticed Zat'tor. A few waved with their tentacles—their hands were busy carrying baskets, strange liquid orbs, and other objects I didn't recognize. Others called out in a high, bird-like greeting.

"Is this the whole village?" I asked.

"The village itself, yes," Zat'tor said. "A few of our siblings are currently out on a quest. They should return in a half-cycle."

"Siblings? Half-cycle?"

I glanced at Jaeyoung for a translator's note, but he shrugged and said, "It's the same word in both our languages. If I had to guess, Maeleons are a gender-neutral society. Instead of brother or sister, they say sibling."

Paz shrugged. "Maybe half-cycle means two weeks, like half a moon cycle?"

I glanced up at the sky, not sure what I'd see. There was the blazing white circle of the sun, eerily similar to Earth's sun. But on the far end of the sky, almost fading into the pale blue, was a crescent moon. Just one. Not two, or three, like other planets. It felt surreal to see a single sun and moon, on top of plenty of water and plant life. How had Eukaria dodged the attention of Earth's scientists? From what I'd seen in a couple hours, this planet was a goldmine of resources—not that I necessarily wanted everyone to know it.

But I recalled the blinking light incident on the ship. When everything was functional, Eukaria wasn't visible anywhere on my star map. We'd only noticed it when all the systems failed. It was literally a hidden gem in the solar system. Who—or what—set that up?

"Come along," Zat'tor encouraged as he strode forward with his long, powerful legs. His tentacle still perched across my shoulders, urging me to keep up with him.

I glanced at my crewmates. They followed, looking less hesitant than I expected. Jaeyoung took in his surroundings with that tell-tale scientist expression that said, 'I could stay and research this forever.' Meanwhile, Paz looked like he was on a tour of a botanical garden. All he was missing was a camera.

Didn't *either* of them care about our imminent demise?

Zat'tor stopped in the center of the village. Suddenly, the mane of weird, fern-like things flowing down the back of his skull began wiggling. Zat'tor raised his head and let out a loud cry. It sounded reptilian, or prehistoric. Whatever it was, it summoned the attention of every Maeleon in the area. They all gathered around us.

Paz and Jaeyoung huddled closer to me, as if finally realizing the gravity of the situation. Either that or they were a bit unnerved by the dozens of seven-foot-tall tentacled aliens encircling us.

"Sibling, what are these creatures?" a brownish-hued Maeleon asked. It and the others eyed us curiously, like cats watching fish in a tank.

I squirmed nervously in Zat'tor's grip, but he gave me a reassuring stroke with his tentacle.

"These are humans," Zat'tor explained, saying the word slowly.

"Where did they come from?" a bright green Maeleon asked.

I took this opportunity to explain ourselves. Clearing my throat, I said, "Greetings, Maeleons. I'm Captain Levi, a human from Earth."

My explanation apparently meant nothing to the Maeleons. They blinked at me as if I'd said a bunch of gibberish. Were the ITMs no longer working?

"Er," I said, unnerved by their silence. "We come in peace?"

The Maeleons took a step closer, unfurling their tentacles all at once. An unintentional yelp of fear escaped me.

This was it. This was the end.

Zat'tor patted my hair again. "My siblings want to explore your body," he explained, as if that was perfectly normal.

Burning heat flooded my cheeks. They wanted to do *what* now?

"That has very different connotations on Earth," I blurted out in a near-shriek.

Zat'tor tilted his head. "You do not want this?"

"No, thank you."

Zat'tor held me closer with his tentacle. "I comprehend. Then only I may touch you."

The other Maeleons backed off. I sighed in relief.

I never recalled giving Zat'tor permission to touch me. He'd just kind of... done it.

And I'd just kind of... not minded it.

That didn't mean I wanted a whole village of Maeleons rubbing me all over, though, so I was glad Zat'tor had intervened. Good to know consent was a thing on this planet.

"What about the fire?" a dark green Maeleon asked. "Do these *hyoomuns* have anything to do with that?"

My stomach plummeted. I'd nearly forgotten about that. How would the others react when Zat'tor told them the truth? Even if he seemed to understand, that didn't mean the others would be.

I was afraid, but I had a duty to report the truth. I took in a deep breath.

"We were travelling to a different location when our spacecraft experienced technical difficulty and crash landed on Eukaria. So yes, we were the cause of the fire," I explained. "I'm sorry. It was a complete accident. We didn't mean to harm any of the plant life."

The Maeleons exchanged glances, but I couldn't read their faces as well as I could read Zat'tor's. Whatever they were thinking, it didn't seem to be in our favor. Or maybe that was my overactive imagination.

I swallowed the anxious lump in my throat. I had to step up.

"Please, if you're going to punish anyone, punish me," I offered.

Paz gasped. "Levi!"

"What are you saying?" Jaeyoung demanded, shocked.

I shook my head. I refused to let them take the fall for my blunder. If being killed here was my fate, I could at least try to save their lives before I went down.

"My crew had nothing to do with the fire," I told the Maeleons. "It was due to my incompetence. It's my fault. Not theirs."

The Maeleons wriggled their feelers, as if communicating silently with each other.

"To harm the Sweetfields is taboo," the dark green Maeleon said gravely.

A yellowish one chimed in. "Yes. Perhaps we should sacrifice this human to restore balance."

"It looks like a carbon-based life form," another added, leaning closer to me. "It would make excellent fertilizer."

Before I could even feel a chill of fear, Zat'tor's tentacle wrapped firmly around me. But it wasn't only his tentacle touching me anymore. He grabbed me with his huge hands and pulled me against his broad, warm chest. My heart fluttered at the confusing gesture.

"No," Zat'tor stated with finality. "This human is mine. He is my filum."

What was that strange word? My ITM didn't translate it.

Wait.

Did he just say I was *his*?

I craned my neck to gape up at Zat'tor in shock. Was he... protecting me?

This feeling was so foreign. I was used to being on my own, forging my headstrong path through life. Nobody had ever stood up for me. Especially not someone so big, and strong, and handsome...

What the hell was I thinking? The guy was an alien, for god's sake. Was he even a *guy?* His concept of gender seemed tentative at best.

The other Maeleons were similarly surprised by Zat'-tor's outburst. Upon hearing it, they regarded me in a new light. Nobody challenged him. They all just accepted it, no questions asked.

I couldn't believe it. No way in hell could it be *that* easy. What was this, some kind of cheesy romance plot?

"So, it's settled," I declared, still convinced this was some kind of trick. "I'll take on the punishment instead of my crew. Whatever it is, lay it on me."

Zat'tor cupped my chin. I swallowed a whimper.

"No one is being punished," he said calmly.

"But what about the taboo? The sacrifice?" In a whisper, I added, "You made the consequences sound terrifying!"

Zat'tor looked amused at my squawking. "That is for intentional harm. Your mishap was an accident, yet you owned up to your mistake. That is brave."

I blinked in disbelief. "So, you're not going to kill me and turn me into plant fertilizer?"

"No," he replied cheerfully.

My knees trembled with relief. If I wasn't leaning my full weight against Zat'tor, my legs would've given out. I didn't know how or why fate turned around, but I just dodged a massive bullet.

All thanks to a hunky teal alien.

"But we are going to clean up your mess," Zat'tor said.

I nodded. Those reparations made sense.

"Wait," I said. "We, as in me and my crew, right?"

"No. You said your crew had nothing to do with the accident," Zat'tor pointed out.

Was the whole Maeleon village going to watch me pitifully return to the scene of the crime?

"Then who's we?" I asked.

Zat'tor looked eager. "Since you are my filum, we will do it together."

There was that word again. But I had no time to get stuck on it. He'd offered to help me with the clean-up. Did that mean we were going to be alone together?

Why the hell did that idea excite me?

"Is my crew going to be okay?" Levi asked. He glanced over his shoulder for the third time as we left the village behind on our way to the Sweetfields.

"They will be fine," I assured him.

He bit his lip. "I don't want them to get hurt because of me."

"No one will hurt them," I promised. "It is as you said. Your siblings had nothing to do with the collision. They are not at fault."

"Oh, they're not my siblings," Levi said.

I gazed at him, my tail curling curiously. "No?"

He shook his head, which seemed to be a human gesture for disagreement. As he did this, his dusty yellow tuft of fur whooshed back and forth.

"Humans reserve the word 'sibling' for blood relatives who share at least one parent," Levi explained.

"But you are the same species, yes?" I asked.

"Well, yeah."

"Then you share ancestors. This makes you relatives. Siblings."

Levi blinked his green eyes. Then the corner of his mouth curved upward. "It's true that we share ancestors somewhere along the line. Like, thousands of generations ago. But for humans, that's not enough shared blood to be considered siblings."

That puzzled me. What a strange outlook on relationships humans had.

Levi must have noticed my perplexed expression. "I guess Maeleons don't have that kind of distinction," he suggested.

"No," I replied.

Leaning forward on my arms, I lowered my body to the ground on all fours until the field of wildflowers tickled my belly. I reached one tentacle towards Levi, beckoning him to join me. Unlike a Maeleon, his body was not built to crouch in a quadrupedal pose, so he bent his knees instead.

"What is it?" he asked.

My tail gently brushed the colorful petals. "Do you see these flowers?"

"Yes."

"Do you think we are the same species?"

Levi's brow creased. "Er, is this a trick question?"

"No."

"Then my answer is no," Levi said, shaking his head. "You're clearly different species."

"Correct. However, we're not *that* different. We both drink the same air, water, and sun."

"You... photosynthesize?" he asked, brows raised.

"You cannot?"

Levi smiled. "Nope. That sounds convenient, though." He turned his attention back to the flowers. "So, you consider these your siblings?"

"They *are* our siblings," I confirmed.

"Right," Levi murmured.

I sat on my haunches to match his pose. "You don't believe me."

He raised his hand, sounding flustered. "I do! It's just... outlandish." As the word came out of his mouth, he grimaced. "Sorry, I don't mean it that way. I should say, it's not what I'm used to."

"Yes. Humans are not what I am used to, either," I agreed.

Levi's lips curled, flashing a slight glimpse of flat teeth. "We're on the same page, then."

I was captivated by his expression. I cupped his cheek with my hand, noting the softness of his pale flesh. But it wasn't pale for long. As I touched him, his skin changed color again, blooming with that pink hue.

"W-what is it?" he asked.

"I like this," I stated.

"Huh?"

"I like what your face is doing right now." I ran my thumb across the impossibly soft skin as it turned deeper and deeper pink. "It makes your eyes shine."

Levi swallowed, even though he hadn't eaten or drunk anything. "Oh. Um, this is called a smile. I was smiling."

"Do it again," I ordered.

"Hey, you can't just order me to smile on command," he grumbled, doing the opposite of a smile.

"Why not?"

"It's considered being *bossy*. For humans, anyway. We don't like being told what to do." He pursed his lips in thought. "Usually. There's exceptions, if you're into that kind of thing..."

"What is *bossy*?" I asked.

Levi thought about it for a moment. "Maeleons have no

concept of bosses, huh? Another way to say it would be overbearing, or domineering."

"And you do not like this?"

Now he didn't seem sure. He blew out a warm breath. "I mean, it's okay when you ask me to smile. I was just surprised to hear you say it." In a quieter voice, he added, "No one's ever said that to me before."

I nodded in an attempt to mirror his human mannerisms. "Then I will continue to dominate you."

Levi coughed. "Wait, what? N-no, not like that."

My tail waved back and forth as I tried to make sense of his confusing statements.

"I do not comprehend," I admitted.

Levi's cheeks continued to flare pink as he stood up and brushed off his body coverings. "Never mind. Anyway, don't we have work to do?"

He was right, though it had slipped my mind because of how much I enjoyed our conversation.

As Levi stood upright, he paused and glanced at the flowers under his feet.

"Um, Zat'tor?" he called.

I loved the way he said my name. "I am listening, Levi."

"Is it okay that I'm stepping on your... siblings?" he asked.

Happiness coursed through me. My feelers floated airily, lifted by my emotions.

"Yes, it's all right," I assured him.

Levi looked slightly relieved, but said, "Are you sure? I don't want to accidentally hurt anything else while I'm on this planet."

"Look down," I instructed.

He followed my gaze to the flowers beneath us. I lifted one of my feet. As soon as my weight was gone, the flowers sprang back into place, like I'd never been there at all.

"Each plant has a different personality," I told him. "These are hardy flowers who enjoy roughhousing."

Levi's brow rose. "They do?"

"Oh, yes. Listen."

I heard the flowers' voices clear as day, but after a few moments of silence, Levi shrugged.

"I don't hear anything," he admitted.

"All things in time," I promised. "Now, let us clean up."

It was hard to miss the oblong silver object strewn in the Sweetfields. The sight of it filled me with discontent, but it had brought Levi to me, so I couldn't be too angry.

Levi's shoulders sagged as we approached the fallen ship. He sighed and ran his hand over the hull. The earlier joy and pink hue on his face were gone. He looked sad, like he'd lost something valuable.

I realized I'd perhaps been insensitive. Levi hadn't understood my relationship with the plants, but I hadn't considered his feelings about this crashed device, either.

"I am sorry," I murmured.

Levi glanced at me, green eyes widening in surprise. "What for?"

"This object. It is important to you."

Emotion wavered in Levi's gaze. "Thank you, Zat'tor. I mean, it's not *that* important." He flashed a half smile, trying to console me. "The important thing wasn't the ship itself, but what it represented." He sighed. "Which has now gone up in smoke..."

"What did it represent?" I asked.

Levi shut his eyes and blew out a breath as if the memory stressed him. "This was my first mission as captain. It was supposed to be easy. I'd lead my crew to the right planet and sign a peace treaty, then head back home. Easy." He ran a hand back through his yellow fur tuft. "That didn't happen. I messed everything up. All because of that stupid blinking light..." He frowned, shaking his head. "No, it wasn't the light. It was me. Because I was too proud to ask for help, I got my crew into this mess."

I didn't understand all of what he said, but that last statement got my attention.

"Do you think being on Eukaria is a bad thing?" I asked.

Levi turned to face me. "Well, if I'd done a better job of being captain, we wouldn't be here."

I didn't like these words. My tentacles responded to my feelings automatically. They curled around Levi's midsection, pulling him closer to me. The bright pink color returned to his cheeks.

"H-hey, what is it?" he stammered.

"You are a fine captain," I insisted. "Whatever that is."

"But I—"

One of my tentacles pressed against his lips, preventing him from speaking.

"No more," I ordered. "Unless you wish to praise yourself, be silent."

Levi made a face, then pulled my tentacle free from his mouth. "Okay, okay, fine. Besides, it's not like I don't enjoy being here. With you."

My feelers rose into the air, buoyed with happiness. "Truly?"

"Yes," Levi mumbled, his cheeks almost red now. "What are those things, anyway? More tentacles?"

"No, these are my feelers," I explained. A few of them floated closer to Levi of their own free will.

He squirmed away from them as if they were offensive. "What does that mean?"

I didn't know how to explain. Feelers were so integral to Maeleons that it was difficult to put into words, much less to a human who apparently lacked them.

"I cannot say. Instead, I will show you. But at a later time. We must clean up first."

"Right. Can't keep getting distracted." Levi put his hands on his hips and examined the crash site. "Um... Now is probably a good time to mention that humans are physically weak."

"I can see that," I remarked.

Levi raised one brow. "Are you making fun of me?"

"No. You are simply very small."

He crossed his arms. "I'm an average male height," he grumbled. He put his hands on the base of the ship and pushed hard. He grunted before giving up. "Dammit. Can you do any better, Zat'tor?"

As I approached the ship, I asked, "What is *dammit*?"

Levi rubbed his head. "Believe me, we don't have time to go into the history of that word right now. Just think of it as a swear word."

"What is a swear word?"

"Maeleons don't swear? Like, using words in a negative way?" Levi countered, looking as baffled as I felt. "You don't say *fuck,* or *shit*?"

"What is negative about sexual intercourse or defecation?"

He grinned, apparently amused. "Never mind. Can you lift the ship?"

I lowered myself on my haunches and slid my hands under the hull.

"You might want to use your tentacles, too," Levi suggested. "It's really heavy. You might hurt your—"

I stood, picking up the ship with ease. It was bulky, but not particularly heavy.

Levi's jaw dropped.

"Wh—how did you do that?" he cried.

"It's lighter than I thought," I remarked, hefting it onto my shoulder.

Levi's eyes were wide. "Wow, Zat'tor. You're strong." He stared at my flexed muscles for a second before clearing his throat and asking, "Are all Maeleons physically powerful?"

"Yes. Are all humans physically frail?" I asked.

He huffed. "Well, we don't like to admit it, but yeah. Most of us, anyway. I doubt even the fittest human body-builder could hold a candle to you." He paused. "Oh, sorry. A candle is—"

"Ah, I know what candles are. We have many back at the village. They are made of golden insectoid wax, yes?"

He tilted his head. "That sounds right, yeah. But with all the plants around, I thought Maeleons wouldn't use candles for light."

"For light? No, no. We use them during intercourse. Many Maeleons like the sensation of hot wax dripping on their skin," I explained.

Levi's face turned deep pink. "I see. You're not shy about that sort of thing, are you?"

"Why would I be shy? Intercourse is natural."

Levi seemed like he was trying to stifle a laugh, but he failed. I liked seeing him this way—smiling, with brightly colored cheeks.

I couldn't resist my overwhelming curiosity. My tentacle stroked his cheek. I was surprised at both its softness and its intense heat.

"You can change color, too," I remarked.

Levi sucked in a soft breath. He froze, then slowly raised his hand to rest on my tentacle. "Yeah. This is called blushing."

"Blushing," I repeated. "I like it."

"Humans blush when we're shy, embarrassed, flustered... or, um, aroused," he mumbled.

That was a wide range of emotional responses.

"I hope you feel aroused," I stated.

That made the color in his cheeks reach his ears. "W-what?"

"I don't want you to feel shame around me," I said, stroking his cheek with my tentacle. "Therefore, I hope you are aroused."

Levi made a strange, choked sound, then began coughing.

"Are you all right?" I asked.

"Fine," Levi said in a thin voice. "I guess I should explain that humans aren't usually so... open when it comes to sexuality."

"Why not?"

"I don't know," Levi stammered.

I tilted my head, examining him closer. "Are you a mature organism?"

He exhaled through his nostrils. "Yes, I'm an adult."

"Do you not enjoy intercourse?" I asked, still confused.

"Yes, I do," he grumbled.

"Then what is the problem?"

Levi bit his lip, gazing off to the side. "I... I don't know. Maybe there isn't one." He swallowed and tucked a fluffy strand of fur behind his ear. "I'm not used to getting hit on."

"I am not hitting you," I pointed out.

"Not *hitting* me," Levi corrected. "Hitting *on* me. It means flirting, or courting."

I moved my head up and down. "Ah. A courtship ritual."

It struck me as odd that no creature had courted Levi in the past. But that was no matter. In the end, he was my filum.

Overcome with fondness for Levi, I rubbed my tentacles across his face. My feelers floated off my neck, also wanting to join in. Every part of my body wanted to be in contact with him, like a shaded plant reaching for the sun.

"Er, Zat'tor?" Levi asked, sounding slightly breathless. "What are you doing?"

"I need to touch you," I replied.

His mouth opened in shock. "You *need* to?"

"Yes."

Levi's lip quivered as my tentacles roamed his head, tracing the line of his jaw, snaking over the planes of his cheekbones, threading through his fluffy yellow fur.

"H-hey, stop that," Levi said halfheartedly. He made no attempt to move, or leave my grip. In fact, he seemed to enjoy it.

"Why?" I asked simply.

For a moment, Levi had no answer. He claimed to want the opposite of his real wishes. Even an eyeless flower could see Levi liked being touched this way.

"We're supposed to be cleaning up the collision site, remember?" Levi asked.

The weight of responsibility dampened my urge for touch. My feelers stopped wriggling, and I removed my tentacles from him.

"You are correct," I admitted. "I apologize for distracting you."

Levi smiled, releasing a small laugh. "No, Zat'tor, it's okay. Don't worry about it." He kneeled and turned his attention to the crushed flowers. "Let's just deal with fixing my mistake first."

"Yes," I agreed.

Levi gave the flowers a sympathetic look. He tried to lift their broken stalks, but it was too late. They crumpled as soon as he removed his support. Levi seemed saddened.

"Sorry, little guys," he murmured. Facing me, he asked, "What can I do?"

"It is all right," I told him. "Now that this ship has been removed, the dead flowers will decompose on their own and turn into fertilizer."

"So, I can't do anything?"

I gave him a warm look. "It is enough that you care. Thank you, Levi."

Levi's eyes fluttered, like he didn't expect the gratitude. "Okay."

As he stood up, I examined him. His body coverings were dirty after kneeling in the ashes. I also noticed that liquid beaded at his forehead and rolled down the sides of his face. It seemed to make him uncomfortable because he wiped it away every so often.

"Phew," Levi said. "Hey, is there a place I can wash off? Like, with water?"

An exciting idea sprang to mind.

"Yes," I said. "I know the perfect place."

CLEANING up the ship's wreckage got me all sweaty and bothered. Not because I actually did any hard labor—my buff alien companion conveniently took care of all that—but because said alien companion felt me up the entire time.

I guessed Maeleons had no concept of personal space, which was strangely okay with me. To my surprise, Zat'tor's tentacles didn't feel *bad*. They were like weird, long massage pillows. With suction cups.

After Zat'tor dropped off the inert spaceship at the village, he led me in a different direction. There was a distinctly worn pathway at our feet, which made me think Maeleons went this way frequently.

"Where are we going?" I asked. "Somewhere popular, I take it?"

"Yes. It is a popular area for Maeleon couples or groups."

I nearly choked. There it was again—Zat'tor's complete frankness when it came to sex. I figured I'd better get used to it. Who knew how often I'd hear him say things like that until we escaped Eukaria?

"So, you're taking me to an orgy spot?" I asked, raising a brow.

Zat'tor apparently hadn't made that connection, so maybe *I* was the one with the mind in the gutter.

"You wanted somewhere with water, did you not?" Zat'tor asked.

I sighed. "Yeah."

His multicolored, fern-like feelers wriggled in the air. I assumed that meant Zat'tor was excited.

"You will like this place," he promised, sounding upbeat. "It is beautiful."

He wasn't lying. When we reached the end of the path, I stared in awe at the gorgeous waterfall in front of us. It overflowed from thickly knotted tree roots into a raised pond bed so clear it looked like it was floating.

I'd seen images of other planets before, but none of them were this beautiful. I hesitated to say it looked like a scene from a movie or video game because it was so *real*. Human minds couldn't have imagined something like this.

"Whoa," I murmured.

Zat'tor examined me, noting my curiosity. "Go ahead. Explore."

Nodding, I walked closer to the edge of the floating pond. I wanted to understand how it worked. I tilted my head, looking at it from all angles and still not getting it. It was outright mystical.

But the closer I got to the pond, the muggier the air became. The earlier exercise had left me sweaty enough, but the heat and humidity here wasn't helping. I wiped the sweat off my brow for what felt like the twentieth time.

"Levi, what does this gesture mean?" Zat'tor asked. He mimed rubbing his arm across his forehead.

It didn't even occur to me that he wouldn't know, but

then again, why would he? We were aliens to each other. Of course our physiology was different.

"So, human bodies do this thing called perspiration," I explained. "In other words, sweat. That's what these little beads of water on my skin are."

"Water?" Zat'tor sounded surprised. "You can create water?"

I shook my head. "Sorry, I should be more direct with my words. It's mostly water, but there's other components in it. It's how human bodies regulate their temperature when it's too hot."

Zat'tor angled his head, intrigued. "You find this temperature too hot?"

I waved a hand dismissively. "Yeah, but it's all right, I'll live."

Suddenly, Zat'tor went shock still. His face hardened, looking serious. "You must," he commanded. "I won't accept any alternative."

That unexpected remark made my heart prance. Was this giant alien worried about me? Hours ago, I expected him to sacrifice my life for plant-kind—now he wouldn't even entertain talk of my death.

I smiled at him. "It was only a figure of speech, Zat'tor. I'm fine. Don't worry."

Zat'tor gave a stiff nod, the tension seeping from his body. His feelers started floating freely again. I had to admit, they were kind of cute. They reminded me of a cat's tail, moving independently of him and secretly conveying his emotions.

On Earth, I'd always been a cat person. On Eukaria, I was becoming a Zat'tor person.

One of Zat'tor's tentacles hovered towards me, stopping in front of my chest.

"If you are hot, why do you not remove your coverings?" he asked. "Are they part of your body?"

He meant my hard suit, the standard spacecraft uniform. The outer shell protected us while the inner layer was supposed to provide basic thermal regulation, but this sauna of a waterfall must be too much for it. So much for technology.

"Ah, no, they're not part of me," I said. Noticing Zat'-tor's curious tentacle, I added, "You can touch it, if you want."

It landed on the top of my chest, then snaked lower. I didn't expect Zat'tor to be so generous with his touching. My heartbeat snagged out of rhythm as Zat'tor's tentacle caressed my lower belly. When it slipped between my thighs, I yelped in surprise.

"Did I hurt you?" he asked, pausing his exploration.

"N-no. You're just being very... thorough."

I saw the gears turning in his head. "Is this area particularly sensitive?"

I felt my cheeks grow hot. It was just my hard suit, dammit. I couldn't even feel anything through it. Why was I getting bent out of shape?

"No," I mumbled. "I mean, yeah, but not with my suit on. Just ignore me."

"That is impossible," Zat'tor said plainly. "How can I ignore my filum?"

There was that word again. I was about to ask what it meant when Zat'tor's tentacle slipped between my thighs and up the curve of my buttocks, lifting me a few inches off the ground with his powerful limb. I gasped.

"You are very light," Zat'tor remarked. "Levi is small and adorable."

I was at a loss for words. Small and adorable weren't

terms I would've used to describe myself. I was an average human male in every sense of the word—average height, average in appearance, and apparently, even less than average as a pilot.

But here was Zat'tor, a hot-as-fuck alien, fawning over me for reasons I didn't understand. No person had *ever* paid this much attention to me on Earth. My profile always got ignored on dating apps, and at gay bars I may as well have been invisible.

And it wasn't like Zat'tor acted this way towards my crew, either. He only paid attention to me. Was I unknowingly exuding some kind of special Zat'tor-attracting pheromones or something?

As quick as he picked me up, Zat'tor set me back on my feet. For a moment the feeling of gravity was odd, like being held in the air by alien tentacles had become my new normal after only thirty seconds.

"Your sweat is increasing," Zat'tor pointed out. "I recommend you remove your coverings so you do not overheat."

Ironically, that made my cheeks burn hotter. But how else was I supposed to react when a huge, attractive guy suggested I strip right in front of him?

I cleared my throat. "Zat'tor, you probably don't know this, but humans tend to be... shy about exposing their naked bodies."

Zat'tor angled his head, his eyes peering curiously at me. "Why? What is under your coverings?"

I huffed in amusement. "Nothing, except me."

"Then why are you shy?" Zat'tor countered. "I am naked."

"Yeah, but you have scales. And..."

Swallowing hard, my gaze drifted to his lower half. He had no exposed genitalia, similar to a reptile. Stupid mammals with our junk hanging out. Why did evolution ever think *that* was a good idea?

"And you, er, aren't... vulnerable like I am," I finished. As soon as the words left my mouth, I knew they made no sense and would only confuse Zat'tor further. I sighed heavily. "Never mind, it's easier just to show you."

I turned around so my back was to him. "Do you see those small red buttons at the back of my neck?"

"Yes."

"Do me a favor and press them."

Could I have done it myself? Yes. But I selfishly wanted Zat'tor to do it. If I was gonna strip in front of an alien, I may as well enjoy myself. Being on the receiving end of his attention filled my chest with a warm, wispy feeling, so why not milk it while I could?

I barely felt the gentle touch of Zat'tor's fingers as he pressed the buttons. My hard suit hissed quietly as the mechanism unlocked and the bulky front plate detached from my chest. I removed it, placing it on the ground, then stepped out of the connected leg pieces.

As I stood there fully nude with my butt facing Zat'tor, my heart hammered in my throat. I couldn't remember the last time I'd been naked in front of anyone, never mind such an attractive individual.

But Zat'tor wasn't human. I had to remind myself of that. He was a Maeleon—as such, he carried no human shame or judgment. He wasn't comparing the way my body looked to supermodels. He had no frame of reference for that, and even if he did, I doubted he'd do it.

Suddenly, I felt the caress of supple skin on my hips. I

inhaled out of instinct, but didn't flinch away. When I glanced down, I saw the fleshy ends of Zat'tor's teal tentacles on my waist.

"H-hey," I said. "What are you doing?"

"You gave me permission to touch you," Zat'tor reminded me. "Should I stop?"

"No," I blurted way faster than I meant to. "I mean, it's okay."

"You are too shy, Levi," Zat'tor mused. "For what purpose do you hide your body, and your emotions?"

As he spoke, he ran his tentacles down my sides. I shivered at the silky sensation. Why did that feel so good?

"I... I don't know," I admitted.

Zat'tor stepped closer to my back. I felt the warmth of his breath against my skin. "Then release that guilt and shame."

I shuddered again. Was it that easy? He made it sound so simple. I bit my lip, unsure if I could let go of years' worth of internalized self-consciousness.

But... Zat'tor's comment wasn't a suggestion, was it? It was more like a command.

If a seven-foot-tall buff alien ordered me to submit to him, how could I refuse?

Okay, Levi, now you sound like an over-the-top damsel, I mentally chided myself.

Still, I tried to take Zat'tor's words to heart. Remembering my pilot training, I let out a long exhale and relaxed my muscles. It was an exercise taught at the academy to steady a racing heart rate. I couldn't say how much it helped though, because as soon as Zat'tor's tentacles roamed to my bare chest, my heart skipped a few beats.

"You are delicate," Zat'tor remarked. "Very soft and smooth, like a flower petal."

I blushed. As a man, I wasn't used to being compared to a flower as a compliment, but it was nice coming from him.

"Thanks," I murmured.

The fleshy suction cups travelled across the plane of my chest. It felt foreign and bizarre, but in a pleasant way. Zat'tor treated me like a precious item. Even in his enthusiasm, he was gentle and slow, never rough or rushing.

My eyelids fluttered shut and I sighed contentedly. Being felt up by his tentacles was oddly soothing. I leaned my weight against Zat'tor's broad, muscular chest, satisfied to let him do whatever he wanted.

If I went back in time and told myself I'd be on an alien planet for one day and already be willing to have a buff alien have his way with me, I would've laughed hysterically. But I was rapidly losing the ability to care. Zat'tor's touch felt good, and he liked doing it. It was a win-win situation.

"There is perspiration all across your skin," Zat'tor pointed out.

I nodded. "It's hot. And... being touched makes me sweat, too."

"Shall we enter the pool?"

I was so distracted by Zat'tor's touchy-feely tentacles that I'd forgotten about the mystical pond. I agreed, wanting to see it for myself and to cool off. Zat'tor wrapped one tentacle around my waist as he led me to the base of the waterfall. He didn't seem to want to break physical contact. That was a nice change compared to some of my past lays who didn't even want me staying the night.

At the base of the falls, Zat'tor stepped into the pool of water. It was light blue with a slight pink shimmer. The colors reminded me of early morning dawn.

"Come," he urged.

I tentatively dipped my toe into the water. It was the

perfect temperature, just the right kind of cold that my body quickly adapted to. The cool waves provided relief from the heat and my feverish skin.

"Does it please you?" Zat'tor asked.

I sighed happily. "A lot of things about this please me."

"Good." There was an inhuman rumble in his voice, like a growl. "I only want to give you pleasure, Levi."

An electric jolt zapped down my spine. Why did he keep saying such sexy things? Was he teasing me, or did he really mean it?

One look into Zat'tor's eyes gave me the answer. They smoldered bright orange as they focused single-mindedly on me. It was honestly a bit overwhelming. Nobody—human *or* alien—had ever gazed at me the way Zat'tor did.

"Why?" I asked, mirroring his favorite question back at him.

Zat'tor blinked. "Why do I want to give you pleasure? Is it not obvious? You are my filum."

Again, my ITM couldn't translate the word.

"You've said that before, but I don't know what it means," I told him.

Zat'tor seemed confused. "I do not comprehend. Humans do not have filum?"

I shook my head. "Nope. My translation device won't even attempt to localize it for me, so I guess there's no direct comparison to humankind."

This took Zat'tor off guard for a few beats. It seemed like I'd just shaken his worldview by not understanding that Maeleon concept. I almost felt guilty, like I was a tourist who'd visited a foreign country and didn't even bother learning how to say 'hello' in the local tongue.

"It is much to explain," he finally said. "I don't know if I can without thinking about it."

"It's okay, don't stress over it." I smiled. "Why don't you, erm... keep touching me instead?"

That was apparently a welcome distraction from his thoughts. Zat'tor swept towards me, his bulky body causing large ripples in the water. My skin prickled with anticipation even before Zat'tor's tentacles caressed my sides. A small moan escaped me as the soft, supple flesh danced across my skin. It was too much to take. Beneath the water's surface, my cock jumped at every touch, invigorated by Zat'tor's attention.

"Oh," Zat'tor said, sounding delighted. "You have a tentacle, too. Although yours is small, and short, and has no suction cups."

My eyes snapped open. When I looked down, I was aghast. My cock had gotten so hard that it poked above the water on full display. My hands flew to cover it.

"Th-that's not a tentacle," I blurted, my face burning hot. "That's my... penis."

"Your penis is very cute," Zat'tor said cheerily.

I would've laughed if I wasn't so mortified. Zat'tor's touches weren't inherently sexual—he was just exploring my body. Had he meant to turn me on, or was I a pervert who couldn't control his libido?

"Actually, just call it my cock," I mumbled, still covering it.

"Your cock is very cute."

My cheeks burned hotter than the fire at the crash site. "Maybe we can stop talking about it."

"Why? And why do you hold your hands over it? I wish to see it."

I reminded myself for the millionth time that Zat'tor didn't feel shame about body parts the way humans did.

Huffing, I lowered my hands, letting my junk hang out in its full glory.

Zat'tor examined it curiously. Not a second later, his tentacle reached for it. I yelped, jumping back slightly.

"Sorry," I said. "I should've told you before, but it's extremely sensitive. It's like, *the* most sensitive body part."

"Does it hurt to touch?" Zat'tor asked.

I gulped, feeling lightheaded. "No. The opposite. It feels really good when it's touched."

This pleased and excited Zat'tor. Without waiting, he snaked his tentacle closer, eager to feel me up.

I don't know what came over me, but I stopped resisting. I realized that I didn't really *want* to hold back anymore. If Zat'tor wanted to make me feel good, why shy away from him? It wasn't exactly like I was a beacon for sexual attention back on Earth.

But it wasn't just the sensations I enjoyed. Beyond his curiosity about my body, it really felt like Zat'tor cared about me for *me.*

I held my breath as Zat'tor's tentacle touched the tip of my cock. The fleshy tendril teased the tip, then caressed the bump of my head, moving down my shaft. The pleasure shooting through my bloodstream was incredible. After only a few moments, my balls ached for release. I must've been really pent up. Either that or Zat'tor's touch had magical alien powers. Honestly, it could've been both.

"You are right, Levi," Zat'tor remarked as he explored my cock. "It is sensitive."

"I told you," I said breathlessly.

Zat'tor tipped his head sideways. "Are you sure it's not a tentacle? It twitches and pulses like one."

The fact that he'd pointed that out was both adorable and embarrassing.

"I'm sure," I said.

Zat'tor stepped closer, pulled by his curiosity. Now my back was against the cool stone of the waterfall. Good thing, too. My knees were about to give out from pleasure-induced weakness.

I couldn't help but moan when the tentacle wrapped around my shaft, engulfing its whole length. My legs shook like jelly, and I whimpered like a virgin. I may as well have been one—Zat'tor's deliberate, sensual caresses made me feel like I'd never been touched before.

I gasped as I felt a second tentacle brush against my balls.

"Zat'tor," I choked out. "I can't take much more."

His tentacles stilled. "Does it hurt you?"

I licked my lips. "No, it's not that. I'm going to... finish."

"Finish what?"

Oh, just spit it out, Levi.

"If you keep touching me, I'm going to orgasm, Zat'tor."

His face lit up like he'd just opened a gift. "Ah! Wonderful."

"Wonderful," I echoed. I was still getting used to Zat'-tor's mannerisms, but his earnestness in wanting to pleasure me was oddly sweet.

"Then I will continue at once," Zat'tor stated, not waiting for me to reply. That was fine with me. As his tentacles worked my cock, I was too dazed with arousal to make good words anyway.

I *was* pent up. When was the last time I took care of myself? Probably the night before the mission when I was too stressed to fall asleep. That was almost a week ago.

I finally gave up and threw away the last shreds of my captain's dignity. Screw it. I was into alien tentacle hand jobs now.

I groaned, bucking my hips into Zat'tor's touch. He made a rapid clicking sound in his throat, almost like a dolphin. I assumed it was a joyful sound because it got louder the more I moaned. His tentacles worked faster, roaming across every inch of my aching cock. Zat'tor leaned in and placed his hands on the smooth stone on either side of my head. He was so close I felt his breath against my face. Being pinned made everything hotter.

My arousal peaked. I cried out as I came. The tentacles squeezed and pulsed around my cock like they were milking every last drop.

Millions of stars flashed in my vision. Was I still flying in space after all?

Then I felt something nuzzling me. I blinked blearily when I came down from the high. Zat'tor's face was pressed against my cheek as he cuddled me like a cat claiming a piece of furniture.

"You made much pollen, Levi," Zat'tor said proudly.

I blushed. Nobody had ever complimented my semen production, nor had they sounded so honestly happy about it. Nobody except him.

"Thanks," I mumbled, patting his scaly cheek. I was so exhausted that I didn't bother correcting the term.

Zat'tor pulled back. "You are weary now. I will carry you back to the village."

My pilot training drill sergeant would've had my ass if he saw me, the mission captain, swooning in an alien's arms like a damsel in distress.

But did I give a shit? No.

"That sounds nice," I admitted. "But can I wash off first?"

"Yes. I will help!"

As I smiled at his wholesome enthusiasm, I felt a tickle in my chest.

There was no way I was crushing on the seven-foot-tall alien, right?

AFTER MY FILUM was clean and dry and covered again, I escorted him back to the village. Taking care of Levi was a wonderful feeling. My blood hummed like an insectoid's buzzing wings, already looking forward to our next physical intimacy. But it was enough being by his side, because every moment we spent together was an intimate one.

Now that he was with me, I would never let him go.

The village bustled with activity. Many of my siblings stood around examining the defunct space craft. Among them were Levi's two human companions.

Not siblings, I reminded myself. I had to make an effort to understand their unusual ways.

"I guess nobody knows what to do with it, huh?" Levi asked, nodding to the ship.

Hearing Levi's voice, his taller companion turned around and frowned.

"Captain, there you are," Jaeyoung said. "Where have you been?"

Levi blushed. It was one of my favorite things his little human body did.

"We went to recover the ship and repair the harm to the Sweetfields," Levi explained.

Jaeyoung arched a brow. "Zat'tor brought the ship to the village two hours ago. Then he ran off again. With you, I presume. So, I'll ask again. Where have you been?"

Levi shuffled on his feet. "We were... sightseeing."

Jaeyoung crossed his arms and stared at Levi. "With all due respect, Captain, I find that hard to believe."

"Why is that?" Levi asked.

The third human, Paz, joined the conversation. He squinted at Levi. "Because you look *way* too happy. Like, the happiest I've ever seen you."

"What?" Levi sounded flustered. "I'm not—I mean, I *am*, but it has nothing to do with anything. What have you two been doing the whole time, anyway?"

"The Maeleons didn't want us to wander, so we've been here in the village," Jaeyoung explained. "It seems you're the only one who was allowed to 'sightsee.'"

As he spoke the last word, he curled both index fingers in the air.

"Yeah, and unlike you, we were trying to figure out how to salvage the ship," Paz grumbled. "Y'know, so we can escape Eukaria and get back to the original mission?"

The human's words sent a cold snap down my spine. My organs felt frigid with anxiety.

"Escape Eukaria?" I asked in a low growl. "What is the meaning of this?"

Paz and Jaeyoung shrank back, unnerved by my question, but Levi put his hand on my arm.

"No, no, it's okay, Zat'tor," he said rapidly. "Nobody's trying to escape."

Paz was baffled. "We're not?"

"What do you mean, nobody's trying to escape?" Jaeyoung demanded. "Captain, you can't be serious."

Levi paused with his mouth hanging open, like he couldn't gather his thoughts. Finally, he stammered, "I mean, not today, right? There's a lot of work to do before the ship is fixed. If it can even *be* fixed."

"You don't sound very enthusiastic about the poor ship," Paz mumbled.

"I'm just being realistic," Levi insisted. "Jaeyoung is our only engineer. If he does manage to repair it well enough to fly again, it won't be overnight. Face it. We're going to be on Eukaria for a while, no matter what."

The other two humans went quiet and exchanged glances.

Jaeyoung sighed. "That's true. It won't be an easy fix."

I cared not for the intricacies of spacefaring. The only thing on my mind was Levi. If anything threatened our future together, I wouldn't stand for it.

"It is settled," I announced. "You humans will stay on Eukaria."

The other two glanced at each other again, but didn't reply.

I searched Levi's face. He didn't seem to agree with his crewmates, but he also didn't insist on staying with me. Was he intent on leaving, too?

That was impossible. He was my filum.

Levi lowered his voice. "Zat'tor, can I talk to you privately for a second?"

I assumed he meant away from his human friends. I nodded stiffly and followed him a few steps away.

"Please don't get upset with my crew," Levi said, his brows pinching together as he gazed up at me. "It's my fault they're stranded here. I don't blame them for wanting to leave."

"I am not upset with them," I told him honestly. "I am upset at the thought of losing you."

He shook his head. "No, you won't. I want to stay." He grabbed my hand, holding it between both of his small pale ones. "It doesn't make sense, but... I want to be here with you."

That was a relief to hear. I'd been concerned Levi shared the other humans' opinions. I could not bear a future without him.

I placed my other hand on top of his, stroking it. "But it does make sense, Levi. We are meant to be one. That's what it means to be filum."

Levi sighed, yet he smiled at the same time. "I still don't know what that means, but I believe you."

I wracked my brain. Every Maeleon was born with an innate understanding of it. How could I explain such a deep concept to Levi?

As I pondered it, one of my Maeleon siblings called out behind us. "Zat'tor! You have returned."

It was Linn'ar. In my mind, I attempted to use the human "pronouns" while referring to my sibling, since I did not think Linn'ar would mind. His dark green scales gleamed beneath the sun. My hands were still holding Levi's, so I reached out to touch the tip of his tentacle with my own in greeting.

"This is my sibling, Linn'ar," I explained to Levi. Turning to him, I asked, "Has everyone decided what to do with the spacecraft?"

It took a moment for Linn'ar to react to my words. As his gaze drifted to our interlocked hands, Levi's ears turned pink.

"Yes. We discussed keeping it as a monument to remember this day, since it is the first time other life has appeared on Eukaria," Linn'ar explained.

"It is?" Levi asked, surprised. "The first time *ever?*"

"That is correct."

Levi blinked. "Then, we're the first-ever newcomers to Eukaria?"

"Yes, human," Linn'ar said.

"His name is Levi," I told my sibling.

"Levi," he echoed with difficulty. It was challenging for him to say, as it was for me, but I was getting used to it. "Good to meet you."

"You too, um... Linn'ar, is it?"

He trilled. "Yes."

I was happy to see Levi getting along with the others. He would fit right in here.

"Zat'tor, there is something else," Linn'ar said. "I overheard the humans will be staying."

Levi looked uncomfortable, like he'd done something wrong. "I'm sorry. We'll try not to be a bother."

Both me and my sibling were confused. Why was he apologizing?

Baffled by his statement, Linn'ar went on as if Levi hadn't spoken. "We wish to throw a feast tonight in their honor," he said.

Levi's jaw dropped. "What?"

"Did you say a feast?" Paz yelled. At the news, he ran over, dragging Jaeyoung with him.

"Yes, a feast," Linn'ar confirmed happily.

Paz looked as confused as Levi. "You mean a feast *for* us, right?" he asked. "Not, uh... *with* us? As the ingredients?"

Jaeyoung sighed. "I think it's clear by now our Maeleon hosts have no intention to eat us."

"Just making sure," Paz said under his breath.

Levi rolled his eyes in what appeared to be a dismissive gesture, then turned to me. "Zat'tor, you don't need to go out of your way for us like this. A feast isn't necessary, really."

"Hey, speak for yourself," Paz interjected, holding his midsection. "I haven't eaten anything but a stick of gum since this morning."

"You *ate* gum?" Jaeyoung asked.

Paz pouted. "Not on purpose. I swallowed it by accident when the ship went down."

Levi opened his mouth to say something when a loud growl came from his body. He blushed and put a hand over his stomach.

"Is your belly angry?" I asked.

"N-no," Levi said. "It just means I'm hungry."

Linn'ar and I looked at each other, equally baffled. Humans were as adorable as they were strange. They always hid their true thoughts and feelings. That was something I needed to overcome with Levi. He needed to learn that I wanted to know his truth, always.

"The feast will commence before sunsleep," Linn'ar said simply, turning to leave. "I must go prepare now."

"I guess we should prepare, too?" Paz asked. "Man, I didn't bring anything nice to wear..."

"You can remove your coverings," I suggested.

Paz's jaw dropped. "And show up to the function *naked?*"

"Why not? It makes no difference to us," I told him.

Paz had slightly darker skin than Levi, but his cheeks

deepened in color all the same. I made a mental note of blushing as a universal human physiological function.

"Guess I'll go find a leaf loincloth or something," Paz mumbled.

I took Levi back to my den. After the eventful day, he was tired. I wanted him to recuperate before the feast.

"You should rest before eating," I suggested.

Levi seemed distracted. He examined my den curiously, looking around the space. Thick, woody roots formed the shell of the dome while a hole at the top allowed light to flow in. Flowering vines crept in through the roots, brightening the den with pops of color.

"This is your den?" Levi asked. "Where's all your, uh... stuff?"

"I do not comprehend."

"Your items. Your possessions."

I shook my head, trying to use his human gesture. "Maeleons do not have possessions. Nothing belongs solely to me."

Except Levi. He was unmistakably mine.

Levi blinked, then laughed. "Maeleons would *not* do well on Earth..." Before I could inquire, he pointed to a thick branch extending horizontally across the dome. "What is this, an exercise bar?"

"That is my bed," I explained.

"Huh?"

"I will show you."

I leapt onto the sturdy branch and nestled my belly against it. Curling my hands, feet and tentacles around the wood, I assumed my usual resting pose.

Levi's mouth was agape. "You sleep like *that?* Like a chameleon? Is that even comfortable?"

"Yes, very." I was amused at his shock. I leapt off the branch, joining his side. "How do you sleep, Levi?"

"Well, usually there's some kind of bed." He sighed. "You don't have mattresses, so I guess it's a bunch of soft materials gathered on the floor. Things like bird feathers, cotton, foam... That sort of thing."

I didn't understand half of what he said, but I knew I had to prepare a bed for him to recharge and rest.

"Please wait a moment," I told him.

I left the den, went to the communal resource center, then returned with my arms and tentacles full of a material I hoped was sufficiently soft. When I placed the light pink pile on the floor, I searched Levi's face for approval.

"Do you like this?" I asked.

Levi got on his knees, touching the pile. "Whoa. It's so soft... What is this?"

"This is kofotta tree fibre," I explained. "Artisans use it for weaving, costuming, and decoration."

Levi smiled in an airy, gentle way. "It's like cotton candy." His smile widened into a grin. "It's perfect, Zat'tor. Thanks."

"Rest now," I ordered. "You need your strength."

Levi hesitated. "I usually, um... sleep naked."

Again with the shame. Why were humans so opposed to nudity? Were they born with body coverings on? Did removing them cause physical pain?

"I have seen you naked before," I reminded him.

Levi chuckled. "That's true. I'd better get over it. Could you press that button again?"

When I did so, the hard suit disengaged from Levi's form. He set it aside. As he kneeled by the kofotta pile, he looked demure and vulnerable. Perhaps that was why he preferred the coverings. Unlike us, humans had no scales. They had no natural protection for their soft, fleshy bodies.

Levi's nude form allured me. I wanted to wrap my arms around him and hold him tight to my chest. I wanted to let my tentacles sliver across the planes of his skin. I wanted my feelers to caress every single part of him.

But my desires had to wait. Levi needed rest.

"Sleep now," I urged him.

Levi blinked at me with half-lidded eyes. He already had one foot in the dream world.

"Okay, but don't let me oversleep," he mumbled, lying down in the pink pillowy pile.

"I won't," I promised. I sat beside his makeshift bed, staring at him.

As Levi got comfortable, he glanced up at me. "Are you going to stay there the whole time?"

"Yes. I will watch over you."

A slow, comforted smile spread over Levi's face. "Okay. Thanks, Zat'tor. See you in a couple hours."

"Sleep well, Levi."

IT FELT like I'd just closed my eyes when a moment later, a large hand touched my shoulder, rousing me.

"Levi. It is time for the feast."

I'd known the voice's owner for less than a day, but it was already familiar and warm.

I rolled over in the cotton candy fluff bed. Zat'tor hadn't moved an inch since I fell asleep. That surprised me. It wasn't like he had any entertainment, either—no books, no games, no screens to explore. He'd stared at me the whole time like *I* was his entertainment.

"Hey," I said, my voice thick with sleep. I yawned to shake it off. "Wow, I needed that."

Zat'tor made a soft trilling sound. "Yes, you did. Are you well now?"

I nodded, sitting up.

Then I recalled I was naked. Again. I always managed to lose my clothing around Zat'tor.

My stomach growled. I was ravenous. When was the last time I ate anything? It must've been last night on the ship when we had dinner. Although calling it 'dinner' implied it was fancier than the reality, which was an unappetizing protein-and-carb cube spat out by the ship's meal machine.

"I'm looking forward to this feast," I said, standing up to stretch.

Zat'tor brightened. "Excellent. I wish to feed you and pamper you until you're fully satisfied."

A pleasant shiver rolled across my skin. How could an alien have such a romantic way with words?

I glanced at my hard suit. Honestly, I didn't want to put it back on since it reminded me of my spectacular failure of a mission, but I had no other clothes.

"Hey, Zat'tor," I said, suddenly thinking of an idea. "You said Maeleons weave and make costumes with this stuff, right?"

I gestured to the pink cotton candy fluff I'd slept in.

"Yes," Zat'tor said. "Do you require such a thing?"

I shrugged. "I'd rather wear that than my hard suit."

Zat'tor left for a minute, then returned with what I could only describe as a pink pair of overalls. Or a onesie.

It was definitely... unique.

"Linn'ar makes these," Zat'tor explained, handing the garment to me.

Was it exactly fitting for a captain? No, but I'd make it work. I was sick of being stuffed into my hard suit like a hermit crab.

I stepped into the onesie. It was slightly large on me since it was made for Maeleons and not humans, but it wasn't awkward to move in. It was made of kofotta fibre, and as such, was incredibly soft. It felt silky against my bare skin. I had to admit, it was seriously comfortable.

"It looks wonderful on you," Zat'tor said, his feelers floating happily. "You are so attractive, Levi."

His genuine compliments made me smile. "Thanks."

Would any human man on Earth tell me I looked hot in a pink onesie? Nope. Zat'tor was special that way.

"Now come," Zat'tor said, taking me by the arm. "It is time to feed you."

When we stepped outside the den, it took my eyes a moment to adjust to the lighting. The last time I was outside, it had been broad daylight, but now the sun was setting. Just like on Earth, the descending sun cast a vivid orange and pink glow. The colors on Eukaria seemed brighter, less muddied somehow.

A long wooden table stood before us, full with food and drink. At least, I assumed it was food and drink. Since Zat'tor told me he slept on a fucking branch, I had to remind myself that Maeleons had their own customs and culture.

When we arrived at the table, all the Maeleons lit up and greeted us. I was surprised by their warmth and hospitality. We humans hadn't done anything to deserve it. Hell, we'd crash landed in their sacred fields and burned their precious flowers. I imagined a thousand different bad outcomes we could've faced if this had been a different planet.

But this was Eukaria, and our hosts were Maeleons. They were odd, scaly, tentacled, and above all, kind. So far, at least. I kept a seed of doubt in the back of my mind just in case the tables turned on us...

"Yo, Levi!" Paz's voice cut into my thoughts.

I saw my crewmates on the opposite side of the table. I hadn't noticed them at first amidst the bustling Maeleons, array of food, and general party atmosphere.

"Hey, guys," I said. "Sorry for disappearing again. I took a nap."

Paz grinned. "Never mind that. What are you wearing?"

"It looks like a kigurumi," Jaeyoung commented.

"It looks like if pyjamas and a dress had a baby," Paz offered.

I sniffed, sitting down on the bench. "I've just been calling it a onesie. Zat'tor said it looks good on me."

"Yes," Zat'tor agreed, taking the spot beside me.

He sat so close that our thighs touched. Did he do it on purpose, or was he just so big he couldn't help it? Either way, I didn't mind. I liked being in physical contact with him.

"Hey, I never said it looked bad," Paz pointed out. "Actually, it looks comfy. Better than our hard suits. Where do I get one?"

Zat'tor waved a tentacle in the air. A second later, Linn'ar appeared.

"Human Paz wishes to have a pink covering, too," Zat'tor explained.

"Well, it doesn't *need* to be pink," Paz said.

"Oh! Certainly," Linn'ar said, his feelers rising in the air. He looked pleased that more of us wanted his art. He turned to Jaeyoung. "Would you like one, too?"

"Erm, no thank you," Jaeyoung replied.

Looking disappointed, Linn'ar turned back to Paz and said, "Perhaps you can pick one after the feast. It's about to begin."

Everybody took their seats. Sitting on my other side was a Maeleon I didn't recognize. He had purple scales and was slightly smaller than Zat'tor.

"Let us begin, Maeleons and humans!" Zat'tor announced.

The rest of the Maeleons let out that dolphin-trill sound in reply, then began eating.

I blinked. There was no formal toast or speech. Everything felt so casual. After all the dull seminars and useless meetings I'd attended on Earth, it was kind of refreshing. What Zat'tor told us earlier seemed to be true. There was no leader here, at least not in the way we humans were used to. There was no one special Maeleon running the show and giving everyone orders. Everyone was equal.

"Levi, are you all right?" Zat'tor asked. "You haven't eaten anything."

"Oh, sorry. I was just distracted."

I looked at the spread before me. Stone plates and woven baskets were full of oddly shaped, fleshy things.

"What are these?" I asked.

"Fruit, I assume," Jaeyoung said, examining an oblong magenta thing. He sniffed it, then took an exploratory bite.

"How is it?" Paz urged.

We watched as Jaeyoung swallowed the bite, then paused. "Sweet, with a little tartness," he finally said. "Pretty good."

If the smart guy gave it the green light, I wasn't waiting any longer. I grabbed the same kind of fruit and took a bite.

Holy fuck, it was divine. The explosion of rich sweetness and sour edge made me moan. Maybe it was because I was starving, but fruit never tasted so good. I scarfed the whole thing down.

Zat'tor smiled, showing off his teeth. "Do you like it?" he asked eagerly.

I nodded. "Ugh, it's so good."

He handed me another. "More. Eat."

I sure as hell wasn't about to refuse. Consuming one of

the fruits kick-started my appetite. Good thing there was a veritable buffet in front of me.

I wolfed down the food. Each time I finished one fruit, Zat'tor handed me another. I felt like a prince lazing in a chair, being hand-fed grapes. I was a total glutton, but I didn't care. Who was I to refuse free food during a feast in my honor?

My anxieties drifted away. As the delicious fruit filled my stomach, I forgot about the crashed ship, the botched mission, and all my other responsibilities. I didn't realize how high-strung I'd felt until the taut string of tension within me snapped and unravelled.

I felt relaxed. I felt *good*.

When was the last time I'd decompressed like this? It had certainly been a while. When I wasn't doing pilot's training or dealing with boring administrative duties, I spent my little downtime worrying about the future. About this very mission.

But now that the worst had happened—crash landing on the wrong planet due to my own negligence—it felt like I could finally *breathe*.

I leaned into Zat'tor's strong arm beside me. His presence was like a balm on my soul. He was just so big and comforting and nice. All he wanted to do was make me happy. I couldn't ask for a better partner than that.

Wait... partner?

We weren't that close, were we? Although he did keep calling me his 'filum,' whatever that was.

My gaze slipped over to Zat'tor. I assumed he'd be partaking in the feast and having a good time, but he was just fondly staring at me.

"Enjoying yourself, Levi?" he asked, smiling.

My mouth was full of fruit, so I nodded. A bit of juice

dripped down the corner of my lip. Without missing a beat, Zat'tor whisked it away with his thumb, then I watched his long tongue lick it off.

An aroused shiver rolled down my spine and pooled straight into my balls.

I sucked in a breath as a sudden realization hit me. My cock was half hard, and getting harder by the second.

What the hell? I thought, stunned.

I stared down at my thighs. There it was, plain as day—my erection tenting the pink onesie.

Heat flooded my cheeks. On top of being horny, I was seriously confused. Except for Zat'tor licking his thumb, nothing had happened. Did the fucking Horny Fairy zap me with her wand?

Maybe if I ignored it, it would go away on its own. I grabbed another fruit and bit hard, taking out my frustrations on it. But as I swallowed the juicy flesh, my cock throbbed as if it had been touched. The sensation startled me. I yelped.

"Is everything all right?" Zat'tor asked.

My heart raced. "Fine," I replied stiffly.

Everything was so not fine. Who the hell got horny eating *fruit*?

Slightly panicking now, I gazed across the table at my crewmates for help. But I noticed something odd. Their faces were flushed, too. They shuffled in their seats, as if sitting uncomfortably, but continued to eat fruit like nothing was wrong.

As I stared at the food on the table, a realization slowly dawned on me.

Did the fruit have an aphrodisiac effect? That explained my random sudden-onset boner.

Sweat beaded my forehead. My face felt hot. I wanted

to shift the way I was sitting, but I couldn't do it without rubbing my cock against my thighs and shooting a burst of arousal through my body.

Did the fruit function the same way for Maeleons, or just us humans?

I glanced curiously at Zat'tor. He looked the same as ever—handsome and sexy.

Fuck.

My balls ached with need. Memories of my tryst with Zat'tor replayed in my head. I craved the feeling of his tentacles wrapped around my cock, milking me for all I had...

My head spun. Obviously, all the blood had rushed elsewhere. I had to get out of here before I passed out.

I stood up from the bench with shaky knees. Trying to keep my voice steadier than my legs, I said, "This has been wonderful, but I need to, ah, go to the bathroom."

Zat'tor's ears perked. He stood up immediately.

"You look unwell. I will help you," he offered.

There was no room for argument. His authoritative tone sent a tingle of pleasure across my skin.

"Okay," I said.

Zat'tor gently took me by the arm and led me away from the table. His scaly hand touching me set my blood on fire. I was short of breath, almost dizzy with arousal. I bit my lip. I was glad we were leaving the feast because my erection was painfully obvious. It strained against the pink onesie like there was a flashlight sticking out of my leg. If I didn't get my needs met soon, I felt like I'd explode.

By the time we reached Zat'tor's nest, my heart was pounding a mile a minute. My skin was hotter and sweatier than a sauna.

Zat'tor stared me down. "You are aroused," he stated.

That much was plain as day.

"Yes," I managed to say. Clearing my throat, I asked, "Are those fruits... supposed to do that?"

Zat'tor looked confused a moment, then nodded. "I forgot to explain our customs. When we celebrate with a feast, it's meant to be followed by sex."

All the blood rushed away from my head and down to my other head.

"Oh," I said meekly.

Maeleons were indulgent creatures, weren't they? Then again, maybe humans weren't indulgent enough. In my current state, I was erring on the Maeleons' side.

I was too horny to think. All I knew was that I needed to be taken care of—*now*.

I licked my lips. "Zat'tor..."

He stepped closer, towering over me with his broad, muscular chest. Raising a hand, he stroked my cheek. The coolness of his scales against my burning hot face made me sigh in pleasure.

"Allow me to take care of you," Zat'tor said. It was half request and half command. There was room to refuse, but why the hell would I ever want to? I *wanted* Zat'tor's touch. More than anything.

Throwing the last scrap of pride to the wind, I closed the space between us, pressing myself against Zat'tor's chest.

"Touch me," I breathed.

When Zat'tor's reptilian eyes flashed, I knew I was about to get fucked silly by an alien.

I'D BEEN WAITING for this moment to make Levi's wish come true.

During the feast, I'd grown more aroused every passing moment. Not because of the fruit's aphrodisiac effects, but because of Levi. Seeing him consume food, watching the juice drip wantonly down his chin, knowing his body was growing hot and electric—it was almost too much to bear. I'd barely contained my urge to throw him on the table and mount him in front of everybody. The only reason I did so was to remain polite for our human guests. My fellow Maeleons, of course, would've cheered us on.

But now I had no such qualms. Levi craved me, just as I did him.

He was my filum, and it was finally time to show him what that meant.

Levi stripped out of the clothing until he was bare. I couldn't keep my claws off him. I grabbed his arms, holding him in place as I examined him. I'd seen him clothing-free at the pool, but this felt different. We were playing around back then. I could tell he wasn't quite ready for the full filum experience. But now I saw it in his beautiful green eyes. He wanted *all* of me.

My hands roamed down Levi's sides. His skin was smooth and hot. I had to be careful of my claws while touching him, since his flesh was as delicate as a flower petal. My tentacles had no such problem, so I draped them across his shoulders, letting their tips explore Levi independently of my hands.

Levi shivered. "Feels nice..."

His cock twitched. It stood hard at what I assumed was its full length. I dropped down to my knees, but even that height was barely low enough to reach Levi's erection. He was my adorable, tiny human.

I parted my maw, heeding my sharp teeth, and slid out my tongue.

Levi sucked in a breath. "Fuck, Zat'tor. Are you going to...?"

He was always so hesitant to say sexual phrases. Maybe I could fuck that hesitancy right out of him.

"I am going to lick and suck your cock," I told him.

Levi made a tiny, flustered sound. "O-okay."

"You want this, yes?"

"Yes!" he blurted.

Then there was no need to wait.

I extended my tongue and began exploring Levi's erection. He gasped as my tongue touched the tip of it, then dipped beneath and ran along its base. Where his cock met his body was a small sac. I'd noticed it before at the pool but didn't examine it at the time. Curious, I probed it with my tongue. That made Levi squeal.

"Sorry," he said, looking embarrassed. "It tickles when you... lick my balls."

I tilted my head. "Is this undesirable?"

He bit his lip. "Um, no. You can keep doing it. I'm just not used to it."

I proceeded gently. Levi continued to squirm, but he was less tense. I wrapped my tongue around the cute sac, enveloping it. Levi shuddered and let out a shaky moan.

"Tickles less now," he said breathlessly. "It feels good, Zat'tor."

Those words were a blessing. I wanted Levi to experience unrivalled pleasure, to unravel beneath my touch.

Angling my maw to avoid touching him with my fangs, I caressed the full length of his cock with my tongue. Levi threw his head back and moaned. His knees trembled and he seemed unsteady on his feet, so I wrapped my tentacles around his midsection to hold him upright.

Levi slowly lost himself to pleasure. My tongue was wrapped around his cock in a spiral, covering most of its surface. He bucked his hips, using my tongue as a device to pleasure himself with.

He tasted divine. The scent of salty sweat and musky human skin filled my nostrils, invigorating my arousal. My blood buzzed like a thousand insectoids were crawling beneath my hide. I sucked him harder, wanting to hear more of those delicious sounds and feel his body's wanton twitching.

Then I felt something warm and soft on my face—Levi's hands. They cupped my jawbone. His touch was gentle, as if he was worried he could hurt me. He was as adorable as ever.

"Fuck," Levi breathed. He was losing himself fully to pleasure.

I tightened the grip of my tongue, milking his cock with it. Levi cried out. His hands clenched my cheeks as he bucked his hips forward, thrusting his small cock deeper into my maw.

"Zat'tor," Levi whimpered, his voice hitching. "I'm gonna—"

His hips moved wildly, rocking back and forth with abandon as his throbbing cock swelled within the spiral of my tongue. Then suddenly, it stopped.

A second passed. Levi's whole body tensed. He threw his head back and let out a guttural sound that echoed in the den. He made no effort to conceal his gratification. His voice was raw and intense, completely undone by my efforts. This pleased me.

A gush of Levi's pollen spurted on the back of my tongue. He bucked and empty himself until his knees trembled with fatigue. Finally, he gasped and lost his balance, but I was there for him. My tentacles wrapped around his chest and hips, keeping him steady as he struggled to catch his breath.

"Oh my god," Levi said shakily. His tuft of blond fur clung to his forehead, and his eyes were unfocused and dazed. "Did you swallow it?"

I assumed he meant his pollen. I parted my maw and unfurled my tongue. His little pool of pollen was still there, held in the concave shape of my tongue.

The sight of it made Levi sway on his feet. I held onto him tightly.

"F-fuck, Zat'tor," he murmured. "That's hot." He bit his lip and paused like he wanted to say something else. "You should, um... swallow it. If you want."

Nothing would come of it, but if it pleased him, I closed my mouth and swallowed his pollen. It had a distinct, interesting flavor. This would certainly not be my last time tasting it.

Levi shivered, then nodded. "Yup. No going back to human sex after this..."

Growling, I stood up to my full height. "You are mine, Levi. I won't allow anyone—human, Maeleon, or otherwise —to mate with you. We are a communal species, but when I look at you, something comes over me. I refuse to share."

Levi's beautiful green eyes went wide as he blinked slowly. A smile broke out over his face and he laughed, stepping closer to me so our chests touched.

"That's fine with me, Zat'tor. I don't want to share you, either," he said.

"I am yours alone," I promised.

Levi's smile brightened, lighting up his eyes. I could tell this mutual display of possessiveness made him happy. Perhaps his human sentiments were rubbing off on me. Normally I would've been opposed to such a thing, but with Levi, I didn't care. He was mine.

"Um," Levi said, suddenly glancing down. He sounded surprised. "This usually doesn't happen..."

Unlike at the pool, where his spent cock turned flaccid, no such thing occurred now. It peeked towards the sky at its full length.

"Please explain," I asked.

Licking his lips, Levi met my gaze. His cheeks were bright red. "I'm already hard again," he admitted.

"Of course you are," I said. "The fruits induce an effect that lasts all night."

"What? All night?" Levi sputtered.

I stroked Levi's damp head-fur. "Does this not please you?"

He thought about it for a moment. "I guess it does, since I'm not ready to stop playing with you yet."

"That is wonderful news—because I'm not even halfway done with you, Levi."

He breathed hard. His hands roamed across my chest, drawing circles. He swallowed, then said, "I want..."

"Tell me," I demanded. "Anything you want, I will give you."

Levi glanced demurely up at me from beneath blond eyelashes. "Zat'tor... I want you to fuck me."

My pulse struck my temple. I'd been waiting desperately for this moment.

The mating urge took over me. Still grasping Levi with my tentacles, I flipped him down onto the soft makeshift bed. He gasped in surprise, but I could tell from his lusty glazed eyes and the scent of his musky arousal that he was excited.

Levi sprawled out beneath me. The flushed pink of his cock contrasted adorably with his pale, creamy skin. He was exposed and vulnerable, on full display for my eyes alone. I wouldn't waste this opportunity to worship his body.

I trailed my tentacles down from his jawline to his chest, over his fuzzy belly, past the hill of his hips, and slid between his thighs. Levi gasped quietly, twitching every so often.

"Zat'tor," Levi murmured.

"Yes?"

His eyes flashed. "Kiss me."

I didn't recognize that word. "What does that mean?" I asked, hoping it was something I could fulfill.

Levi chuckled. "Wait, Maeleons don't kiss? Then I get to teach you. Bring your mouth closer to mine."

I leaned forward so my maw hovered above his flat mouth. Levi's eyes went half-lidded as he parted his lips and pressed them to the tip of my snout. This deeply intrigued me. I let Levi take the lead, wanting to learn from him.

A moment later, his tongue slipped into my mouth. As his tongue brushed against mine, a fiery burst of arousal welled up within me. I instantly understood why he wanted to teach me. The velvety, wet sensation was incredible. It fanned the flames of my arousal, making them burn hotter.

Levi shut his eyes and continued to kiss me. A moan escaped from his soft lips. He angled his head so more of his tongue could explore my maw. I met him halfway, teasing my tongue against his. Mine was longer and thinner, while his was short and flat.

Similar to how I'd sucked his cock, I wrapped my tongue around his and began milking it. Levi moaned loudly and desperately. He clearly liked that. The sound of his pleasure fuelled mine. My cock was close to springing loose from my hidden pocket. Meanwhile, Levi's cock bobbed as he bucked his hips into the air. He was clearly fond of kissing, and now I knew why.

I thought about reaching down with my tentacle to milk his cock again, but I had bigger plans, and they couldn't wait any longer. When I pulled away from our kiss, strings of saliva spanned between us. Levi groaned in pleasure.

"Fuck, that was so hot," he whined. "Did you like it?"

"Yes. I'm going to kiss you more in a moment," I promised. "But I need to fuck you first."

Levi shuddered. "Oh, god, please." His gaze skimmed my lower body. "I don't see your cock. Er, wait, do you *have* one?"

His curiosity was so endearing. "Yes, Levi, I do. But unlike yours, mine isn't always on display. Would you like to coax it out?"

Levi nodded excitely and sat upright. I kneeled beside

him, spreading my legs for him to explore, eager for his touch.

"Is it... here?" he asked, grazing the space between my thighs.

"A little higher."

He moved his hand slightly. "Um... how about this?"

A shiver rippled down my spine. Levi noticed the change in my posture and touched the same area again. This time, all my feelers stood on end. I hissed softly as Levi's thumb grazed horizontally across my wide slit. It was usually hidden from view, but Levi's touch engorged it, making it easier to see.

"That's it," I purred.

Encouraged, Levi stroked the area with great enthusiasm. It didn't take long for the front of my cock to poke out of the slit. I groaned as it met the open air.

"Wow," Levi murmured, staring at it. He let out a small laugh. "Hey, it's not *that* much bigger than mine."

"That's only the tip," I told him.

"Oh."

When Levi's curious hands wrapped around it, a growl tore from my throat. I couldn't even have imagined how good my filum's hands on my cock would feel. Whatever I'd thought, it was a thousand times better. The jolt of arousal pushed my cock out further. It slipped out of my slit like a wyrm emerging from its den.

Levi's eyes widened as more and more of my erection came into view. "Whoa. You weren't lying," he said in awe. "That is *long*."

I blew out a hot breath through my nostrils. "There's more."

"H-how much more can there be? How do you stash the whole thing in there?"

I grunted as I felt the still-inside portion of my cock unfurl. "I suppose Maeleons have different biology."

Levi stared at my erection, eyes wide. His hands explored its length. Each touch of his fingertips sent waves of arousal pulsing through my system. I noticed his own cock throbbing between his thighs. I didn't care if it was the effects of the fruit or just his base natural urges. It felt good to know he was enjoying this, too.

Finally, the entire length of my cock was free. It spanned from Levi's hip to his collarbone, and it throbbed with arousal.

Levi licked his lips as he ran his hand across the top. "Is that it? Tell me that's the whole thing."

"Yes."

He sighed. "Oh, thank god. Any bigger and it'd go all the way through me..." He tilted his head. "Honestly, I have my doubts about this monster fitting inside me at all."

"It will fit," I assured him.

He raised a brow. "How do you know?" Then, with an edge of paranoia, he asked, "Have you fucked a human before?"

"Never," I said gently. I pulled him into an embrace. "You are my first, and only."

That calmed his nerves. "Then how can you be so sure?"

"You are my filum," I reminded him. "Our bodies and souls are meant to be together. It will fit, Levi."

He blushed. "Well, I dunno how your dick is going to defy the laws of physics, but for some reason, I believe you."

I rubbed my cheek against his affectionately. "Let me show you."

Levi lay back against the bed. He gazed up at me with

love and trust. I intended to return those feelings back to him.

I propped my body above his. He looked so small and delicate. Although he was my filum, and therefore made for me, I needed to take it slow until his body adjusted to my size.

My twitching cock loomed over Levi. He swallowed in anticipation. No doubt he was imagining how its length and girth would stretch him.

"Don't be afraid," I said. "I won't hurt you."

He shook his head without taking his eyes off my erection. "I'm not afraid. I'm excited. And curious."

He was ready. I brought the tip of my cock to what I assumed was his entrance.

"Here, yes?" I asked.

His cheeks flushed as he nodded. "Yeah."

It was a tiny, cute hole. No wonder he was concerned about my length. It barely looked big enough to accommodate a human, let alone a Maeleon. Perhaps it was stretchier than it looked.

Levi squirmed and let out soft sounds as I explored the hole. It was pink and had a deliciously musky scent. As the tip of my cock pressed against the hole, it opened up, allowing me inside. My stretchy theory was correct.

"Fuck," Levi whispered. His head rolled back onto the bed and he arched his back. Having something inside him must've been a different sensation than simply stroking his cock.

I wished to explore further. My cock wriggled deeper into the tight hole. I went slow to avoid hurting Levi, but he seemed to enjoy it. He writhed in pleasure, even pushing his hips down to engulf more of my erection. I chuckled, happy at his enthusiasm.

"Feels so good," Levi murmured. "Whatever you're doing, keep doing it."

My feelers floated in the air with giddiness. I loved to see Levi enjoying himself.

Slow but eager, my cock crept forward. I took my time exploring Levi's depths. Every time my sensitive cock brushed against the confines of his tight, hot channel, I fell in love with him all over again. A long purr erupted from my throat.

Levi moaned. His body arched and squirmed as I pushed deeper inside him. Between his legs, his erection pulsed. His green eyes were glazed over, like the sun's reflection on a forest pool. He looked delirious from pleasure.

"I'm going to claim you forever," I promised.

Levi met my gaze, blushing deeply.

"Zat'tor..." he murmured.

I let out a ragged grunt of arousal. "I'm going to fill you to the brim with pollen. Everyone will know you're mine."

A visible shiver zapped through Levi's frame. "A-ah..."

I brought my maw to Levi's mouth. I wanted to kiss him again. He accepted my invitation in a frenzy, crashing his lips against part of my jaw. Our tongues intertwined, swirling around each other. As we kissed, my cock slithered deeper into his hole. Levi moaned louder and bucked his hips wildly. He rapidly lost control. My mating urge roared —it felt like a tangled constellation of roots that started at my heart and shot out through every part of me, taking over until there was nothing left but *lust*.

I grasped Levi's delicate hips, careful not to cut his soft human skin with my claws. I held him steady as my cock penetrated his orifice, stretching him to his biological limits. When I glanced down at Levi's lower stomach, I saw the shape of my erection inside him. It made his belly bulge, and he wasn't even full of pollen yet.

"Zat'tor, please," Levi cried out between kisses. He shoved his tongue into my mouth, demanding more. He no longer held back from his desires. He was utterly unravelled. "Zat'tor, your cock feels so fucking good."

I knew it would. Even with our physiological differences, he was my filum. His body would always accept me.

"Please, cum," Levi begged. "I want to feel your hot fucking seed inside me."

My release was close. But I wasn't going to finish unless Levi did, too.

Still kissing and penetrating him, my tentacles roamed along his body. One wrapped around his straining cock while the other caressed his balls.

Levi melted. His moans turned liquid and raw. He went limp.

"Fuck," he mumbled, the word barely comprehensible. "Please. Breed me, Zat'tor..."

A final shiver ran down my spine.

My feelers all rose. I felt them pulse and shimmer as my orgasm approached. The tangled knot of roots within me expanded, grew, then *exploded*. The hot gush of pollen surged out of my cock and flooded Levi's hole. My cock pulsed—and each time, it rubbed against Levi's ribbed muscle, causing me to ejaculate harder.

Levi screamed with pleasure. His frame tensed and twitched, his channel closing in around me. A white jet of liquid shot out from the tip of his erection as my tentacle stroked it.

The next moments were a blur of pleasure. I remember embracing Levi. I remember his trembling, sweat-damp arms curled around my back. I remember his murmurs of breathy joy. Most of all, I remember the love and joy welling up in my soul, brighter than the sun.

After we were both spent, my cock retracted on its own. It disappeared back into my slit. But it left a considerable amount of evidence behind. Levi's hole quivered as my excessive pollen leaked out of it.

Levi groaned softly from exhaustion. He tried to sit up, but the swelling of his belly prevented it. He blinked at the unusual shape of his body, then his eyes widened to the size of moons.

"Whoa," he said. "Um... That is a *lot* of cum."

"Yes," I purred, content with how cute Levi looked. "I filled you with pollen, just like you asked."

"Pollen, huh? I guess that's what Maeleons call it..." He ran a tentative hand over his stretched belly. Now that the lust-riddled headspace had passed, he seemed embarrassed at his extraordinary size. "God, I look ridiculous," he mumbled with a low laugh. "Like a character in a porn animation or something."

"You look perfect as always," I corrected. I'd hear no such self-deprecating words from my filum.

As Levi adjusted his posture, another gush of pollen spurted out of his hole. He blushed even deeper.

"Is it uncomfortable?" I asked. For Maeleons, that was a normal amount of pollen, but I realized that a human might be sore when experiencing it for the first time.

"Surprisingly, no," Levi remarked. "It's warm. And... it feels good to be full."

I stroked his tuft of blond fur. "Excellent."

Levi smiled as I petted him, leaning into my palm. "Well, I *did* ask you to breed me, so I can't complain about the waterfall of cum. Er, pollen."

My feelers wriggled happily in the air. Did that mean he knew?

I thought to ask him about it, but Levi sighed and nestled against my chest. It was precious how he clung to me.

I decided to discuss the topic later. There was plenty of time. Levi was clearly exhausted, so I laid him down and curled protectively around his small body. I waited until his breathing evened out and I knew he'd fallen asleep before I let the dream world take me, too.

I ROUSED SLOWLY. I didn't want to open my eyes. My bed was so unbelievably soft, and my pillow was so warm. I groaned, not yet wanting to enter the world of the awakened, and snuggled closer to my pillow.

Then I felt the wetness.

I paused. I was a grown man with no underlying health issues. There was no way I'd wet myself in the night. So, what the hell was that?

Before I could muster the courage to wake up and check, a horrible buzzing sound shattered the peace and quiet.

It took me a second to recognize the noise—my UniCom. It was never a pleasant sound, but it felt particularly grating and out of place.

Groaning, I forced my eyes open. I randomly moved my hand around my bed, trying to find it. Usually it was on my nightstand, but—

A rumbling growl came from beside me. From Zat'tor.

It felt like lightning struck me.

That's right, I thought. *Last night, we...*

Without opening his eyes, Zat'tor smacked the UniCom with precision. It flew across the den, smacking against the furthest wall and falling to the ground. The buzzing stopped.

I gaped in both dismay and amusement. Despite the situation, I couldn't help but laugh.

"Zat'tor," I chided gently. "That's a very expensive piece of equipment you might have just broken."

I wasn't too worried. They were built as sturdy as possible to withstand a range of elements. Besides, Jaeyoung and Paz also had their own UniComs, so we wouldn't be stranded if mine broke. Still, I figured I should check it out.

When I tried to stand up, Zat'tor's tentacle wrapped around my waist and pulled me back down.

"Stay here," he mumbled, both petulant and demanding.

I grinned as he forced me to snuggle instead of checking the UniCom.

"That's probably important," I told him. But in all honesty, I could've gone the rest of the day without thinking about work.

"This is more important," Zat'tor argued, resting his chin on my shoulder as he spooned me from behind. I could've gotten out of his grip if I *really* wanted to, but I didn't.

I sighed. "Oh, well. I guess command will have to wait."

"Who is commanding you?" Zat'tor asked. His voice was rough and sexy with sleep. "I'll rip their heads off..."

I snorted. Then I realized Zat'tor didn't know anything about my mission, or why I ended up on Eukaria. From his perspective, I'd just fallen out of the sky one day. I hadn't thought much about my original mission, either, besides the fact that I'd totally botched it. Although, with every passing moment I spent with Zat'tor, that felt less like a failure and more like a blessing in disguise.

The UniCom buzzed again.

From the corner of my eye, I saw Zat'tor glare at it like he had laser vision. Hell, maybe he did. Maeleons were an interesting species.

Instead of zapping it into a pile of soot, Zat'tor sighed and released me.

"Go, if you must, and turn that wretched sound off," he said.

I didn't want to leave his embrace any more than he wanted me to leave, but I'd go if it meant getting our peaceful silence back.

I sighed and finally stood up—and that's when I felt it again.

Gasping, my gaze snapped down to my legs. Thick, golden slime with the consistency of honey trickled down my thighs. It was *everywhere*. There was a pool of it on the lower half of the bed where I'd lain down.

I blinked at it in disbelief. I didn't know what to think. What was that? Had it been *inside* me?

Then a flurry of memories bombarded me. Zat'tor on top of me; Zat'tor's monstrous, slithery cock plowing me; the hot flood of cum that had followed.

My mind put the pieces together. Zat'tor called it *pollen*. The viscous golden fluid certainly looked like it. But there was no doubt. It was alien cum.

Heat rushed to my cheeks. I remembered the unnatural swell of my belly, how fucking *full* I'd been of Zat'tor's cum. Pollen. Whatever. There was so much that it had made my stomach bulge. It was both mortifying and, for some reason, profoundly sexy. Maybe I was a bigger pervert than I thought.

I huffed, smoothing my hands over my belly. It was back to normal now. I don't know what I would've done if it had stayed that way. How could I ever face my crewmates? Their highly ranked captain would be reduced to a horny alien cumdump.

Blushing deeper, I shoved the thought out of my mind. I didn't need a boner first thing in the morning.

The UniCom buzzed incessantly. It was time to shut the damn thing up.

Ignoring the wet feeling running down my legs, I jogged to the other side of the den and picked up the device. It was a small, robust watch-shaped thing. Just before I accepted the call, I swore under my breath. I'd nearly forgotten it had an auto-livestream feature, like a two-way webcam. I quickly ran my hand through my hair in an attempt to look like I hadn't just woken up from the world's most mind-blowing alien sex.

"You're fine, Levi, just a standard call from base," I mumbled to myself.

I put a polite smile on my face and hit accept. The admiral's usual stone-faced expression greeted me. He was a serious middle-aged man with streaks of gray in his clean-cut hair. The last thing he wanted to hear was that his newly promoted captain had just been fucked silly by a foreign life form.

I cleared my throat. "Good morning, Admiral."

"Levi," the admiral said curtly. He paused and narrowed his eyes. "Captain, why aren't you dressed?"

The bottom fell out of my stomach. Shit. A few days on Eukaria and already I'd forgotten how to interact with humans. How could I forget to put clothes on?

"M-my apologies, sir." Trying to sound sincere, I added, "The weather is quite hot here."

The admiral's eyes narrowed further. "You were sent on a mission to an ice planet, Captain."

Goddammit.

I swallowed. "I meant the place I'm currently inside, sir. It's a sauna type of room."

My heart hammered in my throat until he grunted, apparently accepting that story.

"So, you three arrived at your destination," he commented.

His gaze flicked around, examining my surroundings. I kept my back to the wall so he only saw vague darkness behind me instead of the vines and flowers, which contradicted my sauna story.

"Yes, sir," I said. "The peace mission has been going excellently. The locals are quite kind."

Instinctively, I wanted to glance over at Zat'tor, but I didn't want the admiral getting suspicious. I forced myself to keep my focus on him.

The admiral grunted again, which was his way of being affirmative. Probably. It was hard to tell since his grumpy demeanor never changed.

"Hm," he said. "No trouble at all?"

I had a flashback to the whole crashing-the-ship incident, but I kept my face steady.

"No, sir," I replied.

On the other side of the den, Zat'tor slowly stood, yawned, and shook out his feelers like a dog shaking its fur. I held back a smile at how cute he was.

"You know, Levi," the admiral droned on, "this is a simple first mission. I don't expect any major issues."

"Yes, sir," I said absently.

Zat'tor was infinitely more interesting than this administrative spiel. I was spellbound as he rose to his full height and sauntered closer with a hungry look in his eyes. My heart fluttered. What was he doing?

"But in this job, there's always a risk," the admiral continued. "We can never guarantee when locals will be hostile."

I held my breath as Zat'tor stopped in front of me. When I first met him, I'd gotten a literal pain in my neck craning it back to look at him, but I was used to it now. It comforted me that he was so tall and strong.

"Yes, sir," I said, trying not to gaze at the smoking hot alien.

It felt like the admiral wasn't even listening to me. "And what's worse—do you know what's even worse than a hostile local, Levi?"

Fuck. Could he stop asking me questions when Zat'tor's tentacles were reaching out to touch my sides, just out of view of the camera?

"I can't say that I know, sir," I replied.

"Being *lured* by them," the admiral growled. He said it with a dark undercurrent, like it was something unspeakable. "Do you get my drift, Levi?"

Admittedly, I wasn't paying him my full attention. How could I when Zat'tor's tentacles caressed my bare sides? My breath caught in my throat. His smooth, cool flesh sent shivers along my skin. I bit my tongue so I didn't moan on camera.

"Levi?"

Shit. The admiral was still talking to me. I forced my attention back on him while Zat'tor grinned in amusement behind my UniCom screen.

"Yes, sir?"

"Are you paying attention?"

"Yes, sir. The heat and steam are making it difficult to concentrate."

"Well, *concentrate,*" he snapped. "There are dangers on alien planets beyond your comprehension, first timer. As I was saying, being *tempted* by foreign life forms is an even greater danger than violence."

I swallowed as Zat'tor's tentacles snaked down, drawing loose circles across the plane of my naked body. My mind threatened to implode at how good it felt.

"Why's that, sir?" I asked, not caring about the answer.

"Because once you're seduced by the enemy, there's no going back," he stated. "You're on *their* side, not ours. Once you think you're one of them, you turn your back on humanity." In a mutter, he added, "Lost a damn good number of crew members to aliens that way..."

The admiral's tone annoyed me. What did he know about aliens, anyway? All he did was sit in his chair barking orders at everyone and working us half to death.

Suddenly, his words caught up with me, and despite Zat'tor's touch, I snapped back to reality.

"Wait, did you say the *enemy*?" I asked, frowning. "Admiral, we were sent on a peace mission, not one of conflict."

For once, the man looked flustered. It was only there for a brief moment before he went back to his usual grumpy expression. "Slip of the tongue."

Zat'tor's tentacle moved up my body. The end of it reached my collarbone. Before it went any higher, I grabbed it and held it there. I didn't want Zat'tor in the camera field, especially after the admiral's so-called 'slip of the tongue.' I didn't know how the admiral would react if he saw him.

Would he treat Zat'tor like an enemy? I wasn't taking that chance.

"Understood, sir," I said curtly. I wanted to end this call ASAP. "If that's all, may I be dismissed? My crew is pinging me to urgent business."

He grunted, but nodded. "Dismissed, Captain."

When he finally hung up, I sighed loudly and tossed the UniCom to the ground in frustration. I couldn't believe the admiral's rant. He'd never openly expressed sentiments like that before—or maybe he had, and it hadn't struck a personal chord with me because I hadn't *met* any aliens yet. But now that I had Zat'tor, and his 'siblings,' and Eukaria... I couldn't let those anti-alien notions slide.

Zat'tor tilted his head. "What bothers you, Levi?"

"Did you hear what he said?" I asked, riled up. "That arrogant, narrow-minded..."

I trailed off in a huff, too annoyed to speak. I was enraged on Zat'tor's behalf.

Zat'tor didn't seem upset. He gingerly picked the UniCom up with his tentacle and handed it back to me. I glared at the device as if it represented all of the admiral's ugly thoughts.

Zat'tor stroked my hair. "I do not comprehend. Can't you ignore this man?"

I grimaced. "No. At least, I'm not supposed to."

"What do you mean? You are your own being. You are not bound to anyone." His tongue flicked out playfully. "Except me."

I smiled a bit despite my irritation. "Obviously." As the mood came back over me, I sighed. "I dunno. Things are different for humans, Zat'tor. We're always obeying superiors, or barking orders at inferiors. It's not like here on Eukaria."

Zat'tor stepped closer to embrace me. "Your home is here, Levi. You do not answer to anyone except yourself. If that man speaks to you again, I will crush that device to dust."

I chuckled at the mental image—and then I actually thought about it. What if Zat'tor *did* destroy my UniCom? My truest self would be happy never speaking to the admiral or any 'superiors' on Earth again. I could leave all the stress and drama and conflict behind. Besides, the ship was busted, and since the galaxies were so expansive, the UniCom had no location signal. Not unless the captain manually input one. And I had no intention of doing that.

But what about my crew? Was it fair to keep them trapped on this planet because that's what *I* wanted? No, they weren't trapped. Jaeyoung was the most competent person I'd ever met. He'd fix the ship eventually, even if it took a while. Besides, he and Paz weren't chomping at the bit to incite conflict, either. They were both messengers of peace. I was sure they'd understand if I wanted to keep Eukaria a secret from the admiral.

A realization hit me. I suddenly gasped.

"Oh, shit," I said. "The fruit."

Zat'tor made a trilling sound like a laugh. "You want more?"

"No—I mean, *maybe*—but I forgot about my crew. They ate a ton of fruit at the feast, too. Do you think they...?"

I blushed, unsure if I should talk about my crew's arousal. But as usual, Zat'tor had no such qualms.

"I have no doubt they entered a state of heightened lust, yes," Zat'tor confirmed.

I ran to get dressed. "I have to see if they're okay. It's my responsibility as captain."

Zat'tor trailed behind me like a nosy but beloved guardian angel. "I shall accompany you," he announced.

Nodding, I skidded to a halt at my pile of clothes. The

hardsuit lay next to the pink onesie. It wasn't even a choice. The hardsuit felt like an uncomfortable relic of the past, both literally and metaphorically.

I wriggled quickly into the onesie. "Let's go find my horny crew."

Finding my horny crew proved easier than expected. As soon as we rushed out of Zat'tor's den, I saw a group of concerned Maeleons huddled around two adjacent dens. The Maeleons' feelers all floated curiously.

Zat'tor raised his head, parted his mouth, and drank in the air. "I recognize that scent. It's similar to the one you exuded last night."

I blushed furiously. I wasn't used to being told I exuded any scents in a positive way. To my surprise, I also felt a stab of jealousy. I didn't want Zat'tor *scenting* my crew. Only me.

"Come," Zat'tor urged. He took my hand and approached the huddled Maeleons. "Levi wishes to see his fellow humans," he announced.

They parted, allowing us to pass. Two dens, similar to Zat'tor's vine-coated hut, stood next to each other. I assumed Jaeyoung was in one den, and Paz in the other.

My mind raced with thoughts. Did they have Maeleons in there with them? Had they also been fucked silly by aliens? The idea filled me with hope. If so, maybe they'd be in less of a hurry to leave...

"Jaeyoung? Paz?" I called.

At first there was no answer. I hesitated by the doors. I didn't want to barge in, especially not if the effects of the fruit were still active.

After a few moments, Paz called out miserably, "In here."

I entered the hut on the right with Zat'tor trailing behind me. To respect Paz's privacy, I half-covered my eyes with my hand just in case he hadn't fully recovered. But he was mostly dressed in his hardsuit. Dark circles rimmed his usually bright eyes, and his shoulders drooped. He was exhausted.

"Paz, what happened?" I asked sympathetically.

He cast a haggard look my way. "You don't wanna know," he mumbled.

"Trust me, I think I know," I said wryly. "You were unbearably horny after the feast, right?"

Paz squeaked like a mouse. "How'd you—"

"The same thing happened to me. I didn't know what was going on until Zat'tor told me the fruits are an aphrodisiac."

Paz groaned. "Crap. That explains it. And we ate so many of them..."

Glancing around the otherwise empty den, I noticed no signs of another person.

"Were you alone the whole time?" I asked.

He bit his lip. "Yeah. After you left the feast, I started getting... effected. That nice Maeleon who made the onesies —Linn'ar, I think—noticed I wasn't, uh, well. He brought me and Jaeyoung to these huts and asked if we needed help."

"By help, you mean with your arousal, right?"

Paz blushed to the tips of his ears. "Yeah. But I was so embarrassed and freaked out. I asked to be left alone."

I cleared my throat. "So, you took care of yourself?"

"All night long." Paz sighed. "And now I'm tired as fuck."

Zat'tor tilted his head. "Linn'ar would have been happy to assist you. I'm sure any of my siblings would."

Paz looked flustered. "I-I couldn't accept their help. Anyway, Linn'ar seems way more interested in Jaeyoung. I heard him outside all night asking if he needed help, but Jaeyoung kept barking at him to go away."

That was unusual behavior for Jaeyoung. He was always so composed. But this was an unusual situation—not one any of us were prepared for.

"I should check on him, too," I said.

Paz eyed me and Zat'tor. "So, did you two..." He raised a brow, made a circle with his finger and thumb, and slid his other index finger inside in an obvious innuendo.

I blushed profusely. "I'm going to pretend I don't know what you're talking about," I said under my breath, turning to leave.

But Zat'tor apparently wasn't satisfied with my evasion because he proudly told Paz, "Yes, I bred Levi all night long."

"Oh," Paz said, eyes going wide. He tapped his chin and tilted his head, no doubt imagining the mental image. "Huh. And I'm using my imagination here, but does it actually, you know... fit?"

"Absolutely," Zat'tor agreed.

"Goodbye, Paz!" I called as I shoved past the door to stand outside. Huffing, I tried to shake the flustered feeling. Taking alien dick was one thing, but discussing it with my crew mates was another. It was uncouth for a captain.

I paused. Could I even call myself 'captain' anymore? Did I deserve the title? I'd led my crew right into a crash...

As the image of the ship's busted hull flashed in my mind, I asked myself: Did I *want* to crawl back into it and fly back to Earth? What awaited me there? A massive chewing-out from the admiral, first of all. Maybe even dismissal from my position. And what about after? I wasn't looking forward to the soul-sucking loneliness waiting for my return. My parents died when I was a young adult, so I had no remaining family, and I had no close friends, either. I had my crew, but they didn't count. They probably still resented me for crashing on Eukaria and ruining their careers.

Was that why I'd taken on this job in the first place? To escape everything?

I suddenly felt a peculiar warm sensation at the back of my skull. I assumed it was the sun's rays poking out behind the clouds, or more pessimistically, the burn of an oncoming headache.

"Levi?"

Zat'tor's gentle voice pulled me back. He examined my face, searching for answers about why I'd spaced out.

"Sorry, I got distracted," I said.

It was only when Zat'tor withdrew his feelers that I realized it was *him* touching me. He'd never stroked me with his feelers before. What was he doing?

Just as I opened my mouth to ask, Linn'ar approached me with a worried expression.

"Levi! Oh, could you please help us?" he asked.

Poor Linn'ar was as stressed as I'd ever seen a Maeleon look. His feelers were pale and drooped against his back, and his pointed ears lay flat against his cheeks like a sad dog's.

"Sure, Linn'ar, I'll try," I said. "What's going on?"

Beside me, Zat'tor went stiff. He must've instinctively understood his fellow Maeleon's struggle, whatever it was.

Linn'ar fussed with his claws. "It's Jaeyoung. He hasn't spoken to me in hours, and he hasn't come out of the den."

Had the effects of the fruit knocked him out? Or had he jacked off so hard that he passed out? Knowing him, both seemed implausible. If any human could withstand the effects of an alien aphrodisiac fruit, it would be him.

"Have you looked inside?" I asked.

"No," Linn'ar replied sadly. "He scolded me each time I offered to come in."

"How often was that?"

Linn'ar drooped like a wilting orchid. "Every ten minutes until he stopped answering…"

He was probably sick of being bothered, but I didn't mention that to Linn'ar. His concern over Jaeyoung was genuine and wholesome.

"Don't worry. I'll see if he's okay," I told Linn'ar, who brightened instantly.

"Thank you, Levi."

"You two stay here," I said, nodding at Zat'tor. "If Jaeyoung isn't feeling well, he won't appreciate a whole gaggle of onlookers."

Zat'tor made a grumpy, disappointed face but stayed put.

"Hey, I'm coming in," I warned before entering the den.

I didn't know what I expected to see, but it wasn't Jaeyoung folded upside-down with his back against the wall. He was fully dressed in his hardsuit. He was red in the face, sweat trickling down his skin. His brows were knitted together and his eyes were clenched shut.

I blinked in confusion. "Good morning?"

He slowly peeked one eye open. "Levi," he said, his voice hoarse and low.

"Captain Levi," I reminded casually. "So, are you—"

Jaeyoung cut me off with a venomous jab. "If you were a true captain, you'd do a better job getting us off this planet."

My jaw dropped. He'd been curt with me before but never outright rude like this. I was honestly taken aback.

But was he wrong? I hadn't raised a finger to help fix the ship. I didn't *want* the ship repaired.

I stared evenly at Jaeyoung. Like Paz, he had dark circles under his eyes. He'd probably been up all night staving off the effects of the drug. And judging by his strange pose and nasty attitude, I assumed he hadn't given in to temptation. That must've been immensely difficult.

I shrugged. "You're right. I *would* do a better job if I was a true captain. I'm starting to doubt if I even deserve this title. So, I'm not here as your captain. I'm here as a fellow human, and I'll get to the point. Are you okay?"

Jaeyoung unclenched his jaw. My response seemed to disarm him.

"No," he replied. "I am not okay. I'm under the effects of some unknown disease, experiencing ridiculous symptoms and... *urges.*" As he said that last word, he glanced at the door before quickly meeting my gaze again.

I guess he never talked to Paz before they split for the night. Poor Jaeyoung thought he was alone in his erection embarrassment.

I shook my head. "It's not a disease. It's just the fruits we ate last night. They were aphrodisiacs."

His shoulders slumped as understanding dawned on him. "They..." He sighed deeply. "Yes, of course they were."

I shuffled uncomfortably, not sure how to phrase my next question. "Did you ever, er... take care of it?"

"No," he admitted. "Although it's useful to know it's simply a physiological reaction."

He gave another sidelong look at the door, almost as if waiting for somebody. But Linn'ar said he'd shooed him away. I wondered if Jaeyoung was struggling with his urges. He had way more self-control than I did. When I was under the full effects of the fruit, I'd practically begged Zat'tor to plow me.

I quickly pivoted from that thought before it awakened *my* urges again. I cleared my throat. "So, do you plan on trying to fix the ship today?" I asked.

Jaeyoung slowly unravelled from his upside-down position. He stood up and rolled his shoulders. "I might try."

Unease wriggled in my belly. Just thinking about leaving Eukaria made me queasy.

"I see," I said, trying to sound neutral.

Jaeyoung saw right through my efforts. "You don't want me to fix the ship. Is that right, Levi?"

"I didn't say that."

"No. But you're thinking it."

My gaze dropped to the floor. "I don't know," I admitted, rubbing my arm. "I just... I like it here. I like the people and the planet."

"You prefer it to Earth," Jaeyoung said. A comment, not a question.

I exhaled through my nose. "Yes."

It felt good to admit it, but it also frightened me. The rest of my life depended on this choice—but honestly, it wasn't hard to make.

"I think you should wait to decide," Jaeyoung said, not unkindly. "If you were also under the effects of the drug, your choice was made in an altered state of consciousness."

I bristled at that remark. "I felt the same way before I ate the fruit."

Jaeyoung nodded. "Okay. Just think about it, Levi."

I didn't bother correcting him. It honestly felt freeing not to have to be *captain* anymore.

Zat'tor got sick of waiting outside. He waltzed into the den, latching onto my side like a remora on a shark. "Are you finished with your discussion?" he asked.

"Yeah, I think so," I said.

Zat'tor turned to Jaeyoung. "Linn'ar wishes to know if you are well. He is quite concerned."

A fleeting expression crossed Jaeyoung's face. Surprise mixed with something warm. But it was gone as soon as it appeared.

"Yes, you can tell him I'm fine," Jaeyoung said.

"Tell him yourself," Zat'tor replied. Reaching outside with a tentacle, he nonverbally summoned Linn'ar.

The troubled Maeleon rushed inside. The second he saw Jaeyoung, his feelers bloomed. They burst with color and rose shimmering into the air.

"Oh, you're all right!" Linn'ar cried. He looked like he wanted to engulf Jaeyoung in his arms, but held back.

Jaeyoung averted his gaze from the fussy Maeleon. "Yes, I'm fine," he said under his breath. I noticed a dusting of pink across his cheeks, and I didn't think it was from sitting upside-down.

Maybe he was right about waiting. After all, my crew could change *their* minds about leaving, too.

Although I didn't enjoy being separated from Levi while he spoke to his friend, I was pleased to see him in a better mood. Whatever they had spoken about, it must've been uplifting.

Still, I saw none of my siblings in the dens. That was slightly concerning.

"Were your friends all right?" I asked Levi as we departed.

"Yeah. Why?"

"They were both alone, and separated. They did not engage in any intercourse. They must be pent up."

Levi's cheeks turned pink the way they always did when discussing sex.

"They'll be fine," he promised. "Besides, I don't want you to think about them having sex."

He wore a slight frown, as if I'd said something to upset him.

"What is wrong?" I asked.

He huddled closer to me, wrapping his arm in mine. It filled my belly with a pleasant warmth.

"Sorry. It's another stupid human reaction." Levi sighed. "I just got jealous."

"Why?"

He pouted, leaning his head against my arm. "Because I only want you to think about *me* that way."

"Ah. I understand. There is something I have not yet explained."

I stopped walking and gave him my full attention. I wrapped my tentacles around his waist, pulling him as close as possible. "You belong to me, Levi. And I to you. For some Maeleons, it is possible to have multiple filum."

Levi tensed, as if bracing himself for disappointment.

"But not me," I assured him. "You are my one and only filum. I want to have sex with you alone. I only want to kiss *you*. Adore *you*." I brought my maw to his mouth and gave him a light kiss, just like he taught me. "Understand?"

He smiled, his shoulders sagging in relief. "Yeah. Thanks, Zat'tor. I just needed to hear it."

"I will remind you of this fact as many times as you wish. Now, I must feed you breakfast."

Levi chuckled. "Okay, but I am *not* eating any of that horny fruit again for a while."

After I fed Levi a meal that didn't sexually arouse him, he surprised me with a question.

"Hey, Zat'tor," he said softly. "Maybe today... you could teach me some Maeleon customs?"

My heart soared upon hearing those words. It was a blessing that Levi wanted to engage in our culture.

"Yes, beloved," I agreed. "Hmm... I shall take you regenerating."

"What's that?" he asked.

"I'll teach you when we arrive at the site," I promised. "But first, we must acquire a basket and seeds. Let us visit Linn'ar's den."

"If he's even home," Levi murmured in amusement. "It looked like he didn't want to leave Jaeyoung's side."

"Yes, I also noticed that. I suspect Linn'ar feels the same pull towards your friend as I did to you, even if neither of them are aware of it yet."

Levi's brows rose. "You think so? But they've barely spoken."

"Time will pass. They will speak, and get to know each other. If the connection is true, it will happen."

Levi nodded slowly, then smiled. "You sound so confident, Zat'tor. It's funny. If anyone else told me Jaeyoung would fall in love with an alien, I'd laugh it off. But when you say it, I believe you."

I worked my tentacle around his waist as he walked. "It's only a theory based on how Linn'ar looked at your friend. He is not usually so fussy."

Levi grinned. "I guess we'll see."

When we arrived at Linn'ar's den, my sibling greeted us. His mood had improved once he knew Jaeyoung was well. Linn'ar handed us a sturdy basket he'd woven from dry root fibers.

"Are you two going regenerating?" he asked.

"Yeah, although I don't know what that means yet," Levi replied.

Linn'ar trilled happily. "Oh, you will enjoy yourself, Levi! In that case, just wait a moment."

He scurried into his den and returned with a single beige seed. Holding it gingerly between two claws, he placed it in Levi's open palm.

"One for me, one for all," Linn'ar recited. "Now you'd better get going. You will be busy if you're visiting the whole village."

As we went to the next den, Levi faced me and asked, "The thing that Linn'ar said... it sounded like it was part of a ritual."

"You could say that," I agreed. "Regenerating is one of our rituals. We will visit each of my siblings, and each one will give us a seed. We shall take the seeds to the Sweet-fields and plant them where the flowers were crushed."

Levi lowered his face guiltily, but I tipped his chin up.

"It's not a ritual of punishment," I told him. "It's as the name suggests. Regeneration. Starting anew. Feel hope instead of shame."

A smile tugged at Levi's mouth. "I'll try."

We continued our rounds and were rewarded with plenty of seeds for our efforts. Levi gained confidence during each visit as he met and spoke to my siblings, many of them for the first time. Of course, every Maeleon knew Levi was my filum. They treated him as one of our own—which he was.

"You know, this ritual is kind of similar to something we do on Earth," Levi commented. He sorted through the seeds, examining all the different shapes and colors.

"Oh?" I asked.

"On certain parts of Earth, we have a yearly festival called Halloween," Levi explained. "It's mostly for children, but adults can participate, too. Everyone dresses up in a costume and goes door-to-door, kinda like what we're doing. Except instead of getting a seed, you get candy."

"Halle-oh-wiin," I murmured, attempting to say it correctly.

Levi grinned. "That's right."

"Fascinating. What is candy?"

"Oh, they're like small sweets full of sugar." He chuckled. "They're actually pretty bad for you, but they taste good, so humans can't stop eating them."

I imagined Levi stuffing his mouth full of little sweets. The image made my heart clench with fondness.

"Is it like fruit, or honey?" I asked.

Levi tilted his head and hummed thoughtfully. "Not quite. Candy's unnaturally sweet. So, imagine the sweetest honey you've ever tasted. Now imagine it's ten times as sweet and addictive. You could probably eat it until your stomach hurts, and still keep eating it."

That sounded dreadful. But I wanted to experience Levi's culture, too.

"I would like to taste a candy one day," I said.

"Maybe when I go back, I can fetch you some," he replied.

A heavy pause hung in the air. We both felt it. Levi's posture slumped and his mouth curved into a somber frown.

"You said *when*," I pointed out. "Do you intend on returning to Earth if the ship is repaired?"

Levi rubbed the back of his neck. "I was kind of hoping Jaeyoung *couldn't* repair it..."

We were alone on the edge of the village, yet Levi still spoke quietly, like he'd uttered a dark secret.

Discomfort swirled in my organs. A rare feeling cropped up within me: anger. I could've stormed to the ship's wreckage and destroyed it so it could never be used again. But if returning to Earth was what Levi wanted— what he *truly* wanted—then I'd stay my hand.

That didn't stop the growl of irritation buzzing in my throat.

Levi lifted his head. "Zat'tor?"

I swallowed, calming the growl. "I am sorry for my outburst. I despise the idea of you leaving Eukaria."

Levi paused for a moment in thought. "Can I ask you something? Earlier, when we checked on my crew, you touched me with your feelers, didn't you?"

I'd wondered if he noticed that. "Yes."

"I don't exactly know what that means, but... were you worried about me?"

As if they knew we spoke about them, my feelers floated in the air. They itched to touch Levi, to burrow into his mind and senses, to feel all he felt.

"Yes," I said. "I should have warned you beforehand. But I sensed your unease and wished to know why. You should never feel that way with me. My only desires are your safety and happiness."

Levi's expression softened. His green eyes became wet, shining like morning dew. "Zat'tor..." Holding the basket out of the way, he hugged my chest. "You always say the nicest things, you know that?"

"It is the truth," I said, stroking his back. Even now, my feelers crept closer to Levi. But he was not a Maeleon, and didn't yet know their purpose, so I kept them at bay.

Yet Levi was sharp. He noticed the urgent presence of my feelers, even if he didn't understand.

"You can, um... touch me with them. If that's what you want," Levi said.

My heart lifted. He truly was my filum.

"Touching another being with your feelers is more intimate than sexual intercourse," I explained.

Levi blushed, looking even more excited. "Really? Well, I'm ready."

I breathed out as I finally allowed my feelers the freedom they craved. The tendrils moved independently, arching towards Levi like a hundred eager hands. Levi's gaze flitted as he tried to take in each one. Colors danced across my feelers like prisms of light, wild with anticipation.

Levi held his breath as the tendrils vibrated closer. "Is this gonna hurt?" he asked.

"No. I would never hurt you," I promised. "It will feel warm, and possibly strange at first."

When I risked touching him earlier, I didn't get far. I'd barely scraped the surface of his skin before pulling back. But now, I was free to explore.

The tips of my feelers brushed Levi's hair. He shivered. I pressed closer...

A pulse of pleasure ran through me. As the tips of my feelers turned into pure energy and entered Levi's skin, it was nearly orgasmic.

Levi gasped. He blinked, eyes wide. "Whoa."

"How is it?" I asked.

"It's strange, like you said," Levi murmured. "But not bad. It's... warm. Nice. Weird, but nice."

I closed my eyes, allowing pure sensation to wash over me. My feelers, now intangible and ethereal, explored Levi.

Then I felt his emotions.

Anxiety. Worry. Happiness. Guilt. Lust. Curiosity. Love.

Levi didn't want to go back to Earth. He wanted to be here, with me. But he was crushed under the guilt of his error, and concerned his crew wouldn't be able to leave Eukaria because of his mistakes. I understood now why Levi had hesitated.

I withdrew my tendrils. As they exited Levi's body, he shuddered and sucked in a breath.

"That was intense," he murmured, scratching the back of his head. "Were you, uh, poking around in there?"

"Yes. When my feelers enter you, I gain access to your full emotional spectrum," I explained.

He flushed to the tips of his ears. "Oh. That *is* intimate." Biting his lip, he turned his head. "So, you felt all my stress, huh?"

"Yes, and I didn't enjoy it," I admitted. I put my hands on his small shoulders to comfort him. "You do not wish to return to Earth, but you feel sympathetic to your crew. Is that correct?"

Levi sighed. "That about sums it up, yeah."

A weight lifted from my chest. As long as Levi remained by my side, that was all I wanted.

"If your crew wishes to return to Earth, we will do our best to restore the ship," I said.

Levi grinned. "As long as I stay here, right?"

I playfully tickled his ribs with my tentacle. "Yes."

He laughed and pushed it away. "Don't worry about it, Zat'tor. I made up my mind a long time ago."

I kissed him on the cheek, just the way he'd taught me—with my tongue. Levi groaned and wiped the saliva off.

"You can kiss without tongue, you know," he said, amused. He pointed to his cheek. "Try a peck."

I brought the tip of my maw to his soft, peachy flesh.

"That's right," he said warmly. In return, he puckered his lips and pressed them to my snout with a small popping sound. "See? That's a kiss, too."

It was all so fascinating.

After a second kissing lesson, I led Levi to the Sweetfields. We arrived at the site of the crash. With the broken ship removed, the scorched ground was slowly returning to life. I brushed aside the soot with my tail and the remains disintegrated.

Levi kneeled with the basket. "We're planting seeds here, right?"

"Correct. We will regenerate this blackened patch."

The corners of his mouth rose into a smile. "Thanks for teaching me about this, Zat'tor. It makes me feel good to right my wrongs."

"It was an accident," I reminded him. "But it pleases me, too, that you're enjoying this ritual."

I joined him on the ground. Levi placed the basket between us and picked up a single seed. He examined it curiously.

"I'll admit, I've never actually planted something before," Levi said.

"I will teach you. First, we clear a home for the seed," I explained. "Give me your hand."

I took Levi's spare hand in mine and brought it towards the ground. Moving as one, we cleared the remaining dust and soot until fresh soil sprang forth. The soil was damp and ready for a seed.

"Now, place the seed into its new home," I encouraged.

Levi gently set the seed in the hole. "Like this?"

"That's right. Then, we put a roof over its head."

Our hands scraped the soil together, burying the seed.

"Does it need water?" Levi asked.

"Good thinking, Levi. The soil is damp enough right now. We will watch the sky and act appropriately."

We moved as a unit, planting the rest of the seeds until the basket was empty. Levi wiped the sweat off his brow with a soil-stained hand. He flashed a tired but satisfied smile.

"That was really nice," he said, letting out a heavy breath.

I noticed the dampness of his face and the slight yellow

hue eating across his cheeks. I wondered if the physical activity was too much for him. Had he eaten enough earlier?

"Are you feeling all right?" I asked.

"Yeah," he said breathlessly. "Just a little..."

Levi's words tapered off. He went quiet. As his body swayed, I jolted.

"Levi?" I cried.

He shook his head, but as he did so, his cheeks paled. "I'm f-fine..."

That was the last thing he murmured before his eyes rolled back into his head and he collapsed.

My body acted instinctively. My tentacles and arms shot out, grabbing him before he hit the ground. My heart raced at a sickening pace. My organs felt cold, twisted into knots.

"Levi?" I cried when he lolled in my grasp.

No response. Frantic, I bolted upright. Holding Levi firmly in one arm, I crouched on three limbs and raced back to the village.

My memory blurred after planting seeds with Zat'tor. I remembered a sudden dizziness and cold sweat, then the world swayed.

But I also remembered the warm strength of Zat'tor's arms. I didn't see him, but they could only belong to him. I felt safe, despite my sickness. Whatever it was.

When I opened my bleary eyes, I saw the root-swarmed roof of a Maeleon den. I blinked a few times. I didn't feel dizzy anymore, but a strange sensation lingered inside me.

"Levi!"

Zat'tor's voice immediately calmed me. I turned my head to see him kneeling next to the makeshift bed. Concern was written all over his face. I felt bad for worrying him.

"Hey," I said, my voice cracking.

He leaned in, touching me with his tentacles in relief. "I'm so happy you're awake."

"How long was I out?" I asked.

A different voice responded. "A few hours. Zat'tor was in a panic."

I faced the other person, a purple Maeleon I vaguely recognized from the feast. He had a slighter frame than Zat'tor. A basket full of supplies sat nearby.

I suddenly felt a hand touch me—a human hand, not a Maeleon one. When I turned the other way, I saw Jaeyoung frowning with concern.

"Thank god, you're awake," he murmured.

"Is the whole village here?" I said, trying to make a joke. Nobody was amused.

"Zat'tor told us what happened. He said you were fine one moment, then suddenly passed out in the fields," Jaeyoung said. "He ran here as fast as he could."

I nodded. "Yeah, I kinda remember that."

From the corner of my eye, I noticed Zat'tor's tail jerking back and forth in agitation. That must've been a terrifying experience.

"Can you tell me exactly what happened?" Jaeyoung asked. His brow furrowed in concentration as he entered his serious doctor mode.

I thought back, trying to remember anything out of the ordinary. "Pretty much what Zat'tor said," I told him. "We planted a bunch of seeds, and after we finished, I just... passed out."

Zat'tor faced the purple Maeleon. "Healer, would those seeds have a substance that's harmful to humans?"

"I do not know," the healer replied.

Jaeyoung put his palm to my forehead, then shook his head. "You don't have a fever. Is your stomach unwell?"

"Not really."

"Dizziness?"

"Not anymore, no."

Jaeyoung tilted his head, examining my face. "You don't look pale, either."

A frustrated growl buzzed in Zat'tor's throat. "Then, what happened to him? Has the sickness passed?"

I sat up tentatively. Nothing unusual happened. "I think so? I dunno what happened, but I feel fine now."

Zat'tor's tail kept twitching, like he wasn't convinced. He turned to the purple Maeleon. "Healer, we had sex yesterday. Do you think—"

"Zat'tor!" I blurted. Heat flushed across my face. If it was just him and the healer, I wouldn't have minded, but it was awkward in front of Jaeyoung.

The healer made a thoughtful sound. "I did not know. That changes things."

"What do you mean?" Jaeyoung asked.

The healer gave me a long, scrutinizing glance, humming in thought. I sat there awkwardly as he inspected me. What did he see that Jaeyoung couldn't? I was a human, not a Maeleon. Wouldn't a human doctor understand my condition better?

But Jaeyoung seemed perplexed. He followed the healer's lead, looking where he looked and trying to see what he saw. Even Zat'tor joined in.

After a while, I started to feel like an animal on display. "Well?" I prompted. "Anything?"

Finally, the healer grunted and stood. "Please wait a moment."

He went to the back of his den, rummaging around by a window. I turned my attention back to Zat'tor and Jaeyoung.

"Seriously, I feel fine," I insisted. "Maybe I just got heat stroke earlier?"

"I doubt it. The weather wasn't that hot," Jaeyoung said. He paused, then faced Zat'tor. "Why did you bring up the fact that you had sex?"

My face flushed, hard and fast. Maybe now I *would* get heat stroke.

"I pollinated Levi," Zat'tor said seriously. "It is possible he's with child."

A sudden laugh spilled out of me. Oh, poor sweet Zat'tor and his alien sensibilities. He had a lot to learn about human biology.

Instead of laughing, Jaeyoung took the time to explain. "That's not possible," he said simply. "Levi is a cis man. He doesn't have the organs to facilitate a pregnancy."

Zat'tor stared at him like he'd said the moon was made of cheese. "I do not comprehend."

I shrugged. "I can't get pregnant. That's it. There's nothing else to comprehend."

Confusion flitted across Zat'tor's expression as he looked at me. "My cock fit inside you with ease, and your body accepted my pollen. Therefore, you *must* have the organs."

I blushed deeply with embarrassment. I didn't need my resident doctor knowing I'd been flooded with alien cum.

"No, Zat'tor, I don't," I said, trying to be gentle. It was natural that he didn't understand how human bodies worked. "Cis men like me *can't* get pregnant, no matter what. Not even with all the scientific advancements we've made on Earth. It's just a law of nature."

"You asked me to breed you," Zat'tor reminded me.

I coughed, trying to ignore Jaeyoung's presence during this conversation. "Yeah, as dirty talk. I didn't mean literally. It's hot because it can't actually happen."

My explanation didn't convince Zat'tor at all. He stared at me evenly, with the same fondness he always had in his eyes. There was a cool confidence in his aura, like he *knew* he was right. Which was crazy, because he couldn't be.

"Zat'tor, could you explain how Maeleons breed?" Jaeyoung asked. "It might help us understand where you're coming from."

Zat'tor dipped his head. "Yes. Any Maeleons can participate in intercourse, but only filum can breed."

There was that word again. At this point I understood it as a term of endearment, maybe akin to "soul mate," but Zat'tor said it with so much gravity that it felt like something more. Something that sent shivers down my spine.

Speaking of shivers, I suddenly felt the delicate touch of his tentacle on my arm. It was like he couldn't speak about it without being in contact with me. It brought a smile to my face. Almost instinctively, I placed my palm on top of it, like we were holding hands.

Jaeyoung noticed this, but said nothing. He was too immersed in the alien biology lesson.

"So then, not all Maeleons breed. What does being a filum entail? Is it an innate characteristic, or a state of being?" he asked.

I perked up, intrigued now. Leave it to the doctor to ask the real questions.

Zat'tor mulled this over. "It is a state of being."

Jaeyoung stroked his chin thoughtfully. "It sounds like a cyclical phase, similar to estrus in some mammals. Since Maeleons have no concept of sex or gender, I suspect any Maeleon can go into estrus—er, exist as a filum. Is that correct?"

Zat'tor's tail whisked back and forth in concentration, like this was difficult to explain. "Not quite. It is not a state any of us can enter at will."

I could practically see Jaeyoung excitedly taking mental notes. This was his version of an amusement park.

"I see," he said. "What dictates who becomes a filum?"

Zat'tor took a deep breath, closing his eyes as he put his palms on the ground. For a moment it looked like he was praying. When he opened his eyes, he looked straight at me. The fire in his gaze made my heart skip a beat. It was intense, almost supernatural.

I licked my lips. My palm curled tighter around his tentacle. As our skin touched, a familiar tingle lit up below my belly.

Fuck. I couldn't afford to be horny right now, but I couldn't help it, either. Touching Zat'tor was like a drug—stronger than any over-the-counter stuff, or even those aphrodisiac fruits.

"The soil decides," Zat'tor finally said.

Jaeyoung blinked. "The... soil?"

"Yes."

We humans exchanged a glance. Neither of us knew what that meant, but it clearly held weight for Zat'tor. I didn't fully get it, but I figured it had something to do with the Maeleons' relationship with plants. Soil *was* pretty important, after all.

Before we could ask any more questions, the healer waddled back towards us. His hands were cupped together. When he got closer, I noticed he cradled a small, delicate flower on its side. It was naked, with no soil to ground its roots, and its dull gray petals were closed. The poor thing looked dead.

As soon as he saw the flower, Zat'tor sat upright, on full alert. The air around him crackled, charged and eager.

"Levi," the healer said. "Please, open your hands."

I didn't want to stop touching Zat'tor in order to take this wilting flower, but I couldn't be rude by refusing. Reluctantly letting go of him, I held out my palms. The healer placed the gray flower in my hands and stepped back.

Both Maeleons watched with great interest. Jaeyoung, influenced by their curiosity, did the same.

I sighed, back to feeling like a zoo animal. "What's the big—"

Out of nowhere, the flower's roots reached down like tiny fingers and touched my skin.

I froze.

"Uh," I said.

Time stopped. As the flower's roots spread along the surface of my palms, it struck me like lightning that I was on an alien planet. Anything was possible here.

My jaw fell open as the flower continued to move. Its brittle stem stiffened as it rose, standing upright. The drooping leaves happily lifted. And finally, the dull gray petals came to life. They unfurled in a burst of color. The gray drained away in an instant, replaced by bright, healthy pink. The whole withered plant came alive in my hands.

Speechless, I stared at the tiny flower. The den was silent.

"Did... did anyone else see that?" I asked sheepishly.

Jaeyoung leaned in, blinking hard. "How did you do that?"

"I didn't do anything!"

Meanwhile, the two Maeleons grew excited. Zat'tor's feelers danced in the air as a huge grin split his mouth. The healer looked pleased, too.

"That proves it," he said, nodding.

"Proves what?" I asked.

The healer smiled at Zat'tor, who took over. His tentacle curled eagerly around my wrist, like he couldn't resist touching me.

"Levi," he said, voice airy with joy. "You're pregnant."

I almost laughed, but he sounded so damn happy that I

stifled it. I didn't want him to think I was making fun of him.

"Um, okay," I said. "I mean, that can't happen, but if you want to roleplay, I'm okay with that."

From the corner of my eye, I noticed Jaeyoung frowning in thought as he examined the flower in my palms. He wasn't as quick to object to Zat'tor's claim this time.

"Levi, can you give me that flower for a second?" he asked.

I handed it over. I still didn't know why it had bloomed in my hands, but if anyone could figure it out, it was Jaeyoung.

He cupped the healthy pink flower in his hands. The change was immediate. The color fizzled out, leaving only gray behind as the petals drooped sadly. The stem crumpled and fell. The flower looked dead again.

"Fascinating," Jaeyoung murmured. "My hypothesis was that the flower was simply cold, and the warmth of your skin rejuvenated it. But we have the same body temperature, and yet the flower wilted in my hands."

To further test his theory, he asked Zat'tor and the healer to hold the flower, too. It didn't react. Only when the flower returned to my hands did it bloom, healthy and alive. The Maeleons weren't surprised. They acted like this was the most normal thing ever.

Zat'tor inched closer to me. Pure joy radiated from him, making it impossible not to smile.

"What're you so happy for?" I asked with a chuckle.

He angled his head. "Remember, Levi? You are pregnant. This is wonderful news!"

Again with this? I didn't mind going along with it, but he didn't actually think it was real, did he?

"Um, Zat'tor..." I began.

Zat'tor lowered his voice. "Levi. This flower only blooms in the hands of a pregnant being."

I frowned. "What? That doesn't make any sense. How does it know?"

"It's possible the plant reacts to the presence of certain hormones," Jaeyoung mused.

My jaw dropped. "Wait. You're not actually saying this is possible, are you?"

"I just witnessed a flower die and come back to life multiple times," Jaeyoung pointed out. "On an alien planet, is *anything* truly impossible?"

A deep, world-altering shock dawned on me. If the smartest man I knew suggested it was possible, could it be true?

Could I seriously be pregnant?

Levi was quiet for a few moments. If he'd spent his whole life assuming he couldn't bear a child, this must've been quite a surprise. I'd assumed he knew it might happen when he asked me to breed him. It had astonished me to hear both humans insist it wasn't possible.

But it was. Levi was pregnant.

It elated me, yet Levi needed time to process this new information. I would slow down to his pace. Whatever he needed, I would provide.

The den was quiet for a long moment until Levi finally spoke.

"Can we take a walk outside? I need some air," he murmured.

"Of course," I said. Remembering his earlier fainting spell, I asked, "Do you feel all right?"

Levi replied with a smile, "Yeah, I'm good."

I helped him to his feet. The pink color had returned to his face, and his knees no longer trembled, so I felt comfortable taking him for a walk.

"I'm going to stay and speak with the healer," Jaeyoung

said. "I'm fascinated by this discovery. I'll be here if you need me."

Levi nodded wordlessly. Then we exited the den.

I kept a close eye on my filum. He tilted his head back and closed his eyes, letting the sun's rays shine on his face. I smiled. It was probably the baby's influence at work. It needed sunshine to grow.

The daily bustle of the village was comfortable background noise. It was a beautiful day.

After a while, Levi opened his eyes but said nothing. He watched the villagers walk by, going about their lives. There was a peacefulness surrounding Levi, but it was beginning to worry me that he hadn't spoken.

"How do you feel?" I asked, gently looping my tentacle around his waist for support.

He turned his gaze onto me. The green of his eyes was brighter than normal.

"Different," Levi said. "Like... everything has changed." He let out a small laugh, rubbing the back of his hair. "Guess it has, right?"

Wanting to comfort him, I pulled him closer. I couldn't fully understand his feelings since any Maeleon had the ability to get pregnant, given the right circumstances. But Levi had spent his whole existence being told it was impossible for him to bear life.

And now, a tiny seed was growing within him.

He casually walked ahead. I followed him, always in contact.

"Are you frightened?" I asked.

"No," he answered. "Which is weird because I thought I would be."

"What do you mean?"

"I feel like I'm *supposed* to be scared. I mean, what kind

of man wouldn't be freaked out after getting impregnated by an alien on a different planet?" He laughed again, shaking his head. "But it's strange. There's no fear. Hell, I was more scared answering the admiral's call earlier."

My hopes lifted. "Then, you are happy?" I offered.

Levi blinked up at the sky. "Yeah. I think so." He stretched his arms up in the air, then made a content sound. "Man, the weather's nice today. Is the sun always so warm?"

I gestured to his belly with my tentacle. "That is likely the baby's influence. Maeleons need the sun to grow."

Levi's brows rose. He looked down. His midsection looked the same as it did yesterday. There was no obvious growth yet, but there would be soon enough.

Levi curiously ran his hands over his flat stomach. "A baby Maeleon," he murmured. Then he shot me a sassy look. "Hey, what makes you think it won't be a human?"

His snark pleased me. It meant he felt better. After the stressful event in the Sweetfields, I only wanted to see Levi happy and well.

"Do human fetuses thrive on sunshine?" I asked.

"Well, I'm no doctor, but I figure they're not opposed to it," Levi countered.

I grinned. "That is fair."

"What if it's a hybrid baby? Does that happen?"

"As far as I'm aware, no Maeleon has ever hybridized with another species," I mused. "But it might not be outside the realm of possibility."

Levi snorted. "Yeah, that seems to be a theme lately." He took a deep breath. "You know, this all still feels like a dream."

"How so?"

"Crash landing. Winding up on Eukaria. Meeting you." He paused as his cheeks took on a pink hue. "Falling in love with you. And now this. It's just all so—ugh, how do I say this without sounding cheesy?"

"Tell me," I urged.

He blushed harder, biting his lip. "It's... magical."

His aversion to admitting that amused me. Despite all the time I spent with him, I couldn't understand why humans hid their true feelings.

"Why are you ashamed to admit it is magical?" I asked. "If that is how you feel, then it is true."

He made a face. "I dunno. Magical stuff doesn't happen to me."

"Until now."

"I'm not that special. I'm just a *guy*."

I took him by the shoulders, my gaze burning into his.

"You are my filum, Levi," I told him. "You were born to be special. To be *mine*. Your uniqueness is part of you. Do not forget that."

His eyes went soft as the scent of rain. Emotion wavered in them as he murmured, "Zat'tor..."

"If your past on Earth pains you, leave it behind," I urged. "Abandon everything that does not bring you joy. You don't need it anymore."

Levi parted his mouth as if to argue. Then he let out a sigh mixed with a laugh. "You make it sound so easy. Maybe it actually is, and I'm the one making it difficult."

Relief tingled across my skin. Did my words finally get through to him?

Levi tilted his head. "It's not like I have any responsibilities back on Earth. After crashing the ship and disobeying the admiral, I'm definitely relieved of my position." He flashed a wry grin. "Plus, I have a more important responsibility now, don't I? We've got a baby to raise."

A ribbon of delight twirled inside me. I captured Levi in

a blissful embrace. He laughed into my chest, hugging me back. Happiness was a near-tangible force between us, linking our souls and hearts.

"Hey, speaking of babies," Levi mentioned after we parted and continued our walk around the village. "I haven't seen a single young Maeleon since we arrived. All I've met are adults."

"Yes, you have a sharp eye. Currently, all of our youngest siblings are on a journey far away."

Levi perked up. "Oh, right. I remember back when we first arrived, you mentioned something about your siblings being on a quest."

I smiled, pleased he recalled that detail. "Yes. Those are the youngest members of the village."

"I guess since you sent them away, they're not children, but more like teenagers?"

"Nobody 'sent them away,'" I corrected. "They chose to embark on their own. But yes, it is a rite of passage into adulthood."

"Oh, I get it," Levi said, nodding. Then he sharply turned his head. "Hey, is that Paz?"

His friend stood near the edge of the village, staring out into the Sweetfields. He wore a blue onesie, as they called it, no doubt woven by Linn'ar.

"Hey," Levi said again when his friend didn't respond. "Anyone home?"

Paz started. "Huh? Oh, it's you two lovebirds."

"What are you doing here by yourself?" Levi asked.

Paz hummed. "Thought I'd get some air after the whole fruit debacle." He picked absentmindedly at the hem of his onesie. "Do you feel like you're forgetting something? Or like, waiting for something to happen?"

Levi frowned sympathetically. "Not really, no."

Paz sighed, turning back to the field. "Never mind." Suddenly snapping back, he cried, "Oh, shit! I just remembered you passed out earlier."

"How do you know that?" Levi asked.

"Are you kidding? The whole village knows. How could we not, when Zat'tor stormed the place shouting about how you passed out?"

"Oh," Levi said, blushing as he cast a brief glance at me. "I didn't know he did that."

"Yeah, he did. Are you okay?"

"I'm fine, thanks." Levi arched a brow. "Anyway, whatever's on your mind has you messed up, huh?"

Paz rubbed his arm. "I don't know why I'm so distracted. I blame the horny fruit."

I angled my head, examining Paz. The distance in his gaze felt like longing. It gave me the same impression Jaeyoung's expression did when he hid away from Linn'ar. I followed Paz's gaze across the stretch of land. There was nothing on the horizon, but eventually, our siblings would return from there. Not that Paz knew that.

Or perhaps, in his heart, he did.

"By the way, Paz," Levi began awkwardly. "Jaeyoung already knows, so I should probably tell you, too..."

Paz twirled around, eyes filled with curiosity. It was the first time he'd given Levi his full attention since the conversation began.

"Huh? What does he know that I don't? Tell me," he urged.

Levi held up one finger. "I'll tell you, but before you say anything, understand that I'm not lying. This is serious."

Paz danced on the balls of his feet, increasingly enthusiastic. "Yeah, all right, sure, tell me."

Pausing, Levi met my gaze. He seemed to want moral

support, so I put my arm around him and nodded. Meanwhile, Paz glanced between us as if trying to figure out the secret before the big reveal.

"I'm... pregnant," Levi finally said.

Paz's mouth split into a grin, like he was about to burst into laughter, but he suddenly stopped. He must've remembered Levi's warning. His blank face turned into an expression of shock, then powerful curiosity.

"Seriously?" Paz asked, double-checking.

"Dead serious," Levi replied.

Paz looked at me in wide-eyed wonder, as if I'd accomplished a great feat, then back to Levi.

"So, are you trying to be the stereotypical lead in a sci-fi romance, or...?"

Levi sputtered, a flustered blush exploding on his cheeks. "What?"

"C'mon, dude. It's like you crashed the ship on purpose 'cause you wanted to land on the hunky-alien planet," Paz jeered playfully. "*And* you got knocked up to boot? Could you get any more generic?"

"What're you talking about?" Levi choked out. "I didn't do any of that on purpose!"

Paz laughed. "Uh huh, sure. Too bad the ship got messed up, or I'd search your quarters for smutty alien books."

Blushing furiously, Levi spun around and dragged me with him. "C'mon, Zat'tor. Let's leave Paz to his brooding since he wants to make up nonsense..."

A WEEK PASSED since the revelation that I was carrying new life inside of me. By now, my crew knew the truth, and Zat'tor was happily telling anybody who would listen—which, of course, was the entire village. All the Maeleons were ecstatic about the news. Their kindness and attention were overwhelming but nice. On Earth, nobody was excited about my existence, but here on Eukaria, the whole village celebrated me. The difference was night and day.

I'd made up my mind a million times over. I wasn't going back. Not now, not ever.

And that was *before* I found out I was pregnant with Zat'tor's child.

Every morning felt like a blessing. I'd managed to convince Zat'tor to sleep in a soft, comfortable bed with me instead of the weird branch he slept on. Although it didn't take much to convince him. He eagerly agreed to sleep beside me the moment I asked. I adored that about him. He leapt at every opportunity for physical contact, for any sort of connection with me. He *wanted* to be with me, every second of every day.

That was leagues more than I could say for any of the human men back on Earth, which was starting to feel like a hazy memory. Eukaria was my home now, and I liked it that way.

Those fuzzy, happy thoughts floated in my mind as I drifted towards consciousness one morning. I hummed and snuggled closer to the giant alien next to me. Zat'tor slept with his arms and tentacles draped over my side, making me feel safe and snug.

Except, for some reason, I couldn't get as close as I usually did. I squirmed my body to inch towards him.

It didn't work. Again.

Frustrated, I opened my eyes and grunted.

"What...?" I muttered.

Zat'tor was awake instantly, like a car going from zero to a hundred. "What is wrong, Levi?"

"I dunno. I just can't get as comfy as I usually do," I grumbled. "Like something's in the way."

Annoyed that I couldn't snuggle my man, I pulled back and scowled at the space between us.

That's when I saw it—the swelling of my belly.

It felt like the air had been punched out of my lungs. I stared, my jaw dropping. I blinked and shook my head, but it didn't change.

"Levi?" Zat'tor asked when I didn't speak. Then he followed my gaze and saw it, too. He gasped. "Oh, Levi!"

I still couldn't breathe. I was almost afraid to, like if I inhaled, I'd shatter the illusion. But it wasn't an illusion. I wasn't dreaming. This was real.

Finally, because my body grew annoyed at having no

oxygen, I sucked in a soft breath. I reached down with shaky hands. When I touched my own stretched skin, my spine tingled. This was part of me. The baby was in there.

Without warning, tears sprang to my eyes. Emotion choked me as I let out a half sob, half laugh. It was the most wonderful thing I'd ever felt.

"Levi, are you all right?" Zat'tor prompted, his brow furrowed in concern.

"I'm good," I murmured. "Don't worry. It's just..." I trailed off, not knowing how to even finish that sentence. This burst dam of feeling couldn't be put into words. Facing him with tear-streaked cheeks, I smiled. "I'm happy, Zat'tor."

My alien mate mirrored my expression. Then he licked the tears off my face.

"Ew," I said, laughing. "Here, give me your hands."

Zat'tor offered his large, clawed hands. I took them gently in mine, wondering at our differences. His skin didn't feel like human flesh, but it wasn't quite scales either. It was a strange, exotic mix of both that felt deliciously smooth to the touch.

I guided Zat'tor's hands to my newly rounded belly. His expression softened as his palms nestled into the curve.

"So warm," he murmured. He smiled, his shining eyes meeting mine. "So beautiful."

I sighed contentedly, turning into a mushy pile of goo beneath Zat'tor's compliments. I'd never get tired of waking up to his adoring praise.

As Zat'tor caressed my belly, I began to moan. I angled my body as close as possible. His touch felt so good. Maybe there was some Maeleon magic in his palms or something.

"Zat'tor," I murmured.

He made a growl-trill sound that vibrated in his throat. I shivered in anticipation. He was so different than a human man. Every distinct sound and movement he made injected excitement into my blood. How could anyone go back to humans after this?

"Levi," Zat'tor growled softly. "I smell arousal on you."

I blushed. "You're feeling me up. I can't help it."

His tentacles wrapped around my back, cradling me. "I will take care of you."

When he said it, he meant it.

There was no point in refusing him—not that I wanted to. What was better than a loving handjob first thing in the morning? It wasn't like I had any obligations. On Eukaria, I had no strict schedule. I didn't have to leap out of bed at 5 AM to get ready for work. I didn't have to stress about what my boss or co-workers thought of me. I was no longer bound to the soul-crushing capitalist grind of Earth.

I could just *be*.

So, I released a deep breath and let Zat'tor touch me. His supple tentacles followed the curve of my lower back and ass while his hands fondled my cock and balls. My bones felt like they'd turned to jelly. I groaned into his chest.

"Feels so damn good," I moaned, barely coherent. Arousal surged through my veins, making my skin prickle with electricity.

"I would like to try something," Zat'tor said suddenly.

Whatever it was, it was bound to be incredible. "Go for it," I said.

Zat'tor's feelers gently floated into the air, buoying like jellyfish arms as they drifted towards me. My eyes widened curiously. Out of everything, his feelers were the most 'alien' body part. My mind still couldn't comprehend how they'd entered me and felt what I felt. Did he intend to do that now?

My theory was confirmed when the silky tips of Zat'-tor's feelers landed on my body. They were everywhere—my neck, my shoulders, my back, my hips, my belly. I shivered at the delicately soft sensation.

At the same time, Zat'tor also shivered.

"They let you experience my sensations, right?" I asked.

"Yes, and more," he replied. "It lets me match the wavelength of your soul. I feel everything you do, Levi."

I didn't fully understand, but it sounded intimate. And hot. It made me want to do better, to feel more pleasure so Zat'tor could experience it, too.

His large hand stroked my cock while his tentacle groped my ass. At the same time, his feelers wriggled into my body, losing their physical form and turning ethereal. It was like a wild sex dream come to life.

As his feelers latched onto my senses, I gasped and Zat'tor groaned. The tendrils felt like wisps of cloud, or a gentle breeze. My mate felt the same pleasure I did—and I felt *his* mirrored pleasure, too. It was a delicious feedback loop of arousal.

"Levi," Zat'tor growled, his voice gravelly and thick with lust. "Your body is irresistible."

As he spoke, his hand's pace quickened. I whimpered as he milked my cock.

"Fuck," I murmured. My brain was fogged. I couldn't think. Only feel.

Zat'tor was relentless in his touch. While his hand stroked my throbbing cock, his tentacles explored my body. I felt highly sensitive and the satin touch of his tentacles sent jolts along my skin.

I arched my back with a shaky moan, wanting more of everything. Coherent thought was lost. All I knew was pleasure, and that I craved everything Zat'tor could give.

He worked my cock faster. I cried out as hot sensation overloaded me. Although I neared the edge, I felt like I could come and still keep going a thousand times.

A guttural moan echoed in Zat'tor's throat. When something thick and warm pressed against the bottom edge of my belly, I knew without looking down that it was Zat'tor's erection. A shudder rippled down my spine to the base of my balls, making them ache with need. Knowing my mate's pleasure mirrored mine was such a beautiful, erotic feeling.

"Zat'tor," I whispered, too high with lust to speak any louder. "Come with me."

Out of the corner of my eye, I noticed his feelers rhythmically pulsing with color, like neon lights. I took it as a sign of how horny he must be.

I crushed my mouth against his, craving a kiss. He parted his maw and slid his tongue into my mouth. His tongue captured mine, snaking around it and clenching. I moaned loudly. The wet, slick feeling shot straight to my balls.

I moaned Zat'tor's name—or tried to, but with my tongue claimed, it came out as a garbled, wanton mess. I didn't care if I couldn't talk. The mutual pleasure throbbing between our bodies said it all.

Desperation took over me. I moaned and whimpered into Zat'tor's mouth. I bucked my hips wildly, chasing the sweet friction of his touch. I arched my ass into his waiting tentacles. All the while, his feelers writhed within me, reflecting my pleasure and gifting it to Zat'tor.

Suddenly, it all came together. Time stopped. My vision whited out. My body seized. Then I came with an unbridled scream. My orgasm ripped through me like a tidal wave, glorious and powerful. I was helpless to do anything except let pleasure consume me.

And I wasn't alone. The second I came, so did Zat'tor. The mirrored sensations caught up with him and he roared so loud it echoed in the den. His load splashed me, warm and thick, gushing against my belly like the jets in a hot tub. It never seemed to end. It spurted fiercely until Zat'tor's cock finally settled down. By then, his cum pooled in the space between us.

Stars flickered in my vision. I took a few deep breaths until I could see straight again.

"That... was wild," I crackled. My throat felt dry from moaning.

A long purr rumbled in Zat'tor's chest. "It was wonderful."

"That, too."

Zat'tor hugged me closer, paying no mind to the huge mess of cum. That was another thing I loved about him. He was always affectionate, but it cranked up after we fucked. It was like he wanted me to know he loved *me*, not just sex with me.

"I love you, Zat'tor," I said. "Have I ever mentioned that before?"

Warmth spilled across his expression. "Not those exact words in that order. But I already knew."

It was true. We didn't *need* to say the words, but it was a nice little cherry on top.

"And of course, you must know that I love you, too," Zat'tor said, affectionately pressing his nose to mine.

My heart fluttered. I knew, obviously, but it was wonderful to hear it. The words had an especially precious quality coming from his slightly accented Maeleon tongue.

"I do," I told him, nuzzling him back. "Now, uh… maybe we can deal with this pollen situation."

Zat'tor chuckled, eyeing the honey-thick pool with amusement. "As you wish."

ONCE THE STICKY situation was cleaned up, we headed into the village. Levi wanted to talk to Jaeyoung about his pregnancy. Now that his body was visibly changing, he seemed a bit nervous. As much as I reassured him he would be all right, I knew it would be different coming from a trained healer.

Since learning about Levi's condition, Jaeyoung spent much of his time in the healer's den. He was hungry for knowledge, a trait I found admirable. He and Fhi'ran had become friends, bonding over their shared interests.

Levi walked hesitantly into the den. The healers, engaged in a heated discussion about herbs, stopped when they saw Levi.

"Wow," Jaeyoung said, eyes widening. "You look different."

Levi blushed. "I know."

Jaeyoung approached him, examining his changes. "I'm shocked you're showing this much. It's only been a week. Fhi'ran told me Maeleon gestation is quick, but this is unheard of."

Levi rubbed his arm and glanced nervously up at me. I held him closer.

"Sorry," Jaeyoung said, his expression softening. "I wasn't trying to make you nervous."

Levi huffed. "It's hard *not* to be when you're a big pregnant man carrying an alien baby that's apparently growing at hyperspeed."

"The baby's growth is rapid," Jaeyoung agreed, "but I haven't seen any alarming signs. You haven't felt any sickness or discomfort lately, have you?"

Levi shook his head. "Aside from carrying this new weight, no. Not even morning sickness."

"Then I'm not concerned. You seem as healthy as ever." Jaeyoung grinned. "Maybe even healthier. You're even developing a tan."

"I'm outside in the sun a lot more lately," Levi confirmed. "Zat'tor said the baby needs it."

"My sibling is correct," Fhi'ran said. "Maeleon young crave sunlight. It can even speed their development."

Levi snorted. "Does that mean I can pop this thing out ASAP if I sunbathe for a week straight?"

"As a scientist, I would be interested in the results," Jaeyoung said wryly. "But as your doctor, I'm going to suggest you don't do that."

"Noted." Levi angled his head. "So, you're really not worried?"

"If I was, I'd tell you. Fhi'ran, I trust you have no concerns, either?" Jaeyoung asked, facing him.

"I do not," Fhi'ran said. "I am eagerly awaiting the little one's arrival."

Levi smiled, the corners of his eyes wrinkling. He placed his hands delicately on his belly. The fabric of

Linn'ar's onesie stretched over it. I suspected Linn'ar would need to weave more soon.

"Us, too," he said. "I never thought I'd have kids until now—or that it was even possible to carry a baby—but here we are."

A sudden blaring noise shook the den. I scowled. I remembered that foul sound from when Levi's Earth device went off and summoned the facsimile of a man who'd grouched at him.

But it wasn't Levi's device ringing this time. He'd turned it off and left it that way. Either that or it was broken.

Jaeyoung jolted at the sound. He pulled his own device out of his pocket, swearing under his breath. He pecked at it with his fingers until a screen came up, featuring the same grumpy man from before. However, the man's cheeks were now an inflamed shade of purple. He didn't look happy to see a familiar face.

"Admiral," Jaeyoung said in greeting.

"What in the hell's going on over there?" the man spat.

Levi shrank from the vicious demand, huddling closer to me. I tightened my grip on my filum. How dare this screen-man make him feel unsafe?

Jaeyoung didn't react to the rude greeting. "Whatever do you mean, sir?"

"Your *captain* hasn't contacted base in over a week," the man roared. "Where is he? What the hell is he doing?"

A deep growl vibrated in my throat. The way he spoke about Levi was despicable. Why did he think he was so superior to him? Was this normal back on Earth?

"Captain Levi is diligently making connections with the locals," Jaeyoung said evenly. He didn't mention the crash, so I assumed he was playing along with the original mission

Levi mentioned earlier. I respected his ability to remain calm in the face of that brute. "That was the point of our peace mission, was it not?"

That didn't calm the man's fury. "He has a duty to report his findings in a prompt manner," he ground out through his teeth. "He shouldn't be making a *doctor* do his job for him. And where the hell is Paz? I've been calling him nonstop since this morning!"

Levi's face screwed up in confusion, but he didn't interrupt. He went out of his way to avoid being in the angry man's field of vision. I squeezed his shoulder to remind him I was there for support.

"I was unaware, sir," Jaeyoung replied. His calm responses contrasted starkly with the admiral's overreaction. "I'll find him and report back."

"You'd better. I can't have two-thirds of the team going AWOL on me."

"I assure you we are all working hard on our mission," Jaeyoung said.

Even the hotheaded admiral couldn't complain in the face of such a confident statement. He huffed. "Fine. See to it that you do."

When the grumpy man disappeared, Jaeyoung sighed and rubbed his temples. "Good grief. What a hassle." Noticing Levi's slumped posture, he asked, "Are you all right?"

"Can we talk outside? I need some air," Levi replied.

We exited the den. I kept close to Levi, who seemed nervous, but I didn't know why. That brutish man was gone now. Still, Levi's anxiety pulled me in. I wrapped my arm around his shoulders and slid a tentacle around his waist for support.

In my peripheral vision, I saw Paz approaching. Neither

of the humans noticed, and I didn't want to interrupt, so I said nothing.

Levi took a deep breath and faced his friend. "I'm not going back to Earth. Ever."

Closer now, Paz stopped mid-step. "Did I choose a bad time to show up?"

Nobody spoke. Jaeyoung's brows rose, yet his placid expression implied that he wasn't entirely surprised.

Levi took their silence as invitation to continue. "Talking to the admiral is like pulling teeth. I'll be glad if I never talk to him again. Besides, he doesn't even *want* peace. The last time I spoke with him, he 'accidentally' called non-human people our enemies. And he was terrified about everyone seducing us. He's a misguided, ignorant fool."

Jaeyoung and Paz exchanged a glance.

"Are you aware that the admiral has been buzzing your UniCom all morning?" Jaeyoung asked mildly.

Paz shrugged. "Yeah. It got annoying after the first couple times so I turned it off."

"So, you deliberately ignored him."

"Pretty much."

"And I assume you never once thought to answer it," Jaeyoung said, knowing it was true.

"No, 'cause all he does is talk *at* you until he's red in the face. Levi's right, it gets old."

Levi's tense shoulders relaxed. He looked like he'd been ready for an argument, but Paz's comment disarmed him.

"Wait," Levi said. "You guys aren't mad?"

"Why would we be mad?" Paz asked, brow furrowed in confusion.

"Because... I don't want to return to Earth," Levi admitted. "I'm a horrible captain. I refused direct orders, and I'm abandoning our mission."

Paz flashed a lopsided grin. "Well, you're not the most *competent* captain, Mr. Flashing-Red-Light, but you're wrong about the other part."

"Huh?"

"Our true mission, regardless of the admiral's beliefs, was to make peace with life on other planets," Jaeyoung pointed out. "And that is exactly what you've done. Look around."

Levi blinked, then followed Jaeyoung's sweeping gesture. Surrounding us were my fellow Maeleons going about their days. Each one paused to smile and wave at Levi as they passed. It was clear from their sparkling, curious eyes that they were eagerly awaiting the birth of our baby.

Levi turned back to his friend. After a moment, he asked, "But what about the ship?"

Jaeyoung shrugged. "What about it? No one's forcing you to board on the return flight—and that's *if* I can even fix it. It might be damaged beyond repair."

He didn't sound particularly upset. I suspected Jaeyoung was so enthralled by Fhi'ran's local healing techniques that the ship hadn't even crossed his mind lately.

Paz put his hand on Levi's shoulder. "Yeah, man, chill out. You're pregnant, remember? You gotta take it easy."

"Like you've been doing, Paz?" Jaeyoung asked wryly.

"Hey, I've been busy," Paz argued. He didn't elaborate. "Sure."

It was obvious to me that Levi's comrades fully supported him, yet he refused to accept their acceptance. It was like he was afraid to be happy.

He shook his head. "Aren't you going to tell me that the

hormones are influencing my decision or something?" he challenged Jaeyoung.

Jaeyoung almost looked offended. "Hormones or not, your decision has always been the same. You've wanted to live on Eukaria since the day we arrived. Am I wrong?"

Levi's jaw dropped. "I... No."

"I rest my case." He offered a smile. "Levi, nobody thinks less of you for wanting to live here. You have a mate. You're about to have a baby. You're *happy* here. Why would we want to interfere with that?"

Levi slowly raised his head. His eyes watered with emotion. "I don't know... I just figured you two would think less of me."

Paz snorted. "Why, because you found a hot husband and got knocked up? Isn't that, like, the goal for a ton of people on Earth anyway? You just happened to do it on a different planet. One that's kinda awesome."

It pleased me to hear Paz speak of Eukaria that way. It was clear to me that both of Levi's friends enjoyed their time here, too. And they weren't alone. I felt it in my bones that somewhere on Eukaria—in this village or outside of it— their mates were waiting for them.

"Thanks, you guys," Levi murmured. "But what are we going to do about the admiral? We can't just keep ignoring his calls forever."

"I can," Paz interjected.

"And I sure as hell can't tell him I'm pregnant," Levi continued.

Paz tilted his head. "Okay, yeah. What if we lie and say we got abducted?"

"No," Levi said immediately. "I won't reinforce the admiral's beliefs that every other life form is an enemy."

As he spoke, he pressed into me. I smiled and stroked circles in his side with my tentacle.

"True. I guess faking our deaths is out of the question, too?" Paz offered.

Jaeyoung clicked his tongue dismissively. "Too dramatic."

"What if we all gave him the cold shoulder and stopped answering his calls?"

Levi snorted. "That's not very diplomatic of you."

"Hard to be diplomatic with douchebags," Paz argued.

"That's literally your job."

"I'm on vacation."

"Since when?"

"Since my captain crash landed us on a tropical-vacation-central planet."

"Can we stop bringing that up?" Levi grumbled.

"Wait, Levi," Jaeyoung said, thoughtfully rubbing his chin. "What did you say earlier about us being seduced?"

Levi rolled his eyes. "Ugh, that. The admiral went on this tirade about how being seduced by other life forms was worse than hostility or violence. He thought it was the worst-case scenario because the crew would be 'brainwashed' and lost forever." He paused, eyes going wide. "Oh. I see."

Paz cackled. "Wait, are we seriously telling the admiral that we all fell in love with Maeleons and won't be going back?"

The idea seemed to amuse him, but he didn't sound opposed to it. I recalled the way Paz had stood on the edge of the village, as if waiting for someone's return. Did his heart know the truth even if his mind didn't?

"That's the thing. The admiral won't *want* us back if he

thinks we've been seduced," Levi told him. "He'll assume we're a lost cause."

Jaeyoung nodded along. "And therefore, won't risk resources trying to retrieve us. It's perfect."

"I don't want to namedrop the Maeleons, though," Levi said. "This planet wasn't on the GPS, remember? Nobody knows about it except us and the people who live here. I want to keep it that way."

"That's fair," Jaeyoung said.

Paz perked up. "So, we're doing it? We're all pretending to be lovestruck, pregnant himbos with no more space-military usefulness?"

"You seem strangely eager about this," Levi remarked.

"Hell yeah, I am! Who doesn't love lying to their soon-to-be-ex-boss with no consequences?"

Jaeyoung sighed and pulled out the device from earlier. "No better time than the present. Are we all ready?"

"Ready," the other two agreed.

"What should I do, Levi?" I asked.

He frowned thoughtfully. "I don't want you to be in the shot... at least not your face."

"Won't it be more believable if the admiral sees Zat'tor's chest or something? He doesn't exactly look human, so it'd make our story more plausible." Paz grinned. "Especially with how he's always feeling you up."

Levi bit his lip, glancing up at me with concern.

"Do not worry about me," I said, stroking his cheek. "I would do anything to ease your stress, Levi. If this puts an end to your anxieties, I'd be glad to assist."

He sighed. "Fine. Let's get this over with. Call him."

Jaeyoung nodded, then pressed a button on the device. Within seconds, the same translucent screen popped up.

The man they called Admiral glared at Jaeyoung for no discernible reason.

"What?" he demanded.

"Sir, I've gathered Levi and Paz," Jaeyoung said. He panned the screen so the man could see them.

The admiral's veins nearly popped out of his head. "There you are! Where have you been? Status report!" He stopped suddenly, narrowing his eyes at the screen. "Levi, what in the hell is that behind you?"

Levi hesitated, but Paz seized the opportunity with ease.

"Oh, Admiral! That's our sexy new overlord!" he crooned, pitching his voice higher.

The man grunted. He seemed taken aback by Paz's random shift in behavior. "What?"

"Mm, isn't he so hot?" Paz said, batting his eyelashes at me. I assumed this was part of their ploy.

The admiral sputtered. "W-what's gotten into you?"

Paz licked his lips. "Mm, nothing but long, hard, thick *alien*—"

"Enough!" the admiral shouted. "Captain, control your underling!"

"Oh, but I couldn't," Levi said in a lilting tone. "You see, I'm just as obsessed with our... overlord."

"This joke of yours isn't funny," the admiral snapped. "Status report, now!"

"It's no joke, Admiral," Jaeyoung chimed in. He leaned into Levi's shoulder and put on a sultry expression. I almost wished Linn'ar was here to see it. "We're all doting subjects of our new overlord, and we love it this way. Don't we, everyone?"

"Uh huh," Paz agreed with a wink.

The admiral blanched. The change in his color was

shocking. I'd only ever seen him red-purple with rage. Now he was pale, like he was about to faint.

"What's going on?" he demanded. "Jaeyoung, you were fine last time I spoke to you!"

"Ah, I couldn't resist the overlord's temptation anymore," Jaeyoung purred. "I'm sorry, Admiral. I tried for so long." He patted my chest in a platonic fashion. "His powerful teal muscles are just too alluring..."

The scene amused me. I was happy to stand here and be a prop for the humans' theatrics. If this convinced the Earth man to leave them alone, that would be the perfect outcome.

"No, no, this can't be happening," the admiral muttered, sweat dripping down his brow. "I can't lose another damn crew this way!"

"Aw, c'mon, Admiral, you should join us," Paz suggested, wriggling his behind. "Our overlords would *love* to have you."

The man looked like he was about to be sick. He waved a hand as if summoning somebody, then muttered, "Mission 298 has been compromised. Scratch it from the record."

Paz leaned closer to the screen. "What's that, Admiral? You wanna taste of our overlord's juicy cock, too?"

Encouraged by his friends, Levi chimed in, "I can attest it tastes *so* good."

I chuckled behind him. I couldn't help myself. Besides, it appeared their scheme worked. The admiral saluted the humans, muttered some kind of prayer, and terminated the call.

Paz burst into laughter. "Holy shit, that was incredible! I wish we could do that again!"

Jaeyoung ran a hand through his hair, smiling. "That went better than I expected. Good job, everyone."

"Yeah, including you." Paz elbowed him playfully. "Your sultry voice is hot. I've never heard you talk like that before."

"And you never will again."

Levi let out a heavy sigh of relief. "Wow. Is it really over?"

"Did you see the look on the admiral's face? He looked like he was about to cry!" Paz cackled. "It's 'cause he'll never have a taste of that c—"

Levi blushed, cutting him off. "That's enough of that."

Paz arched a brow and laughed. "Hey, you brought it up."

"I was trying to sound believable," Levi grumbled.

"It worked. I totally believed you. Zat'tor is a lucky guy."

"Yeah, well, if *you* ever find a hot Maeleon, you'll know what it's like," Levi teased.

Paz paused for a second, then huffed as if he'd been challenged. "Maybe I will. Just wait and see. What about you, Doc?"

"I'm not the romantic type," Jaeyoung said, waving a hand dismissively. Before Paz could pursue the subject, he turned to Levi and said, "It's been a long day for you and your little one. You should get some rest."

Levi placed his hands on his belly. Every time he did so, his eyes lit up.

"Yeah, good idea," Levi said. "And... thanks, you guys. Really. I wouldn't have been able to face him without your help."

His friends smiled at him. I felt the bond between them shimmer like morning dew. I was glad to know that despite being far from Earth, he'd always have the best reminders of it with him—here in his new home.

DEALING with the admiral was a load off my mind. I could finally let all my anxieties drift away. With no more past to bog me down—and no more guilt that my friends resented me—I was free to throw myself into my new life as a member of the village, as Zat'tor's mate and our baby's father.

Jaeyoung was right about the baby's rapid growth. If a human baby ever grew this quickly on Earth, it'd be an international incident. But here on Eukaria, it felt strangely normal—which was something I never thought I'd say, because nothing about a cis man getting pregnant with an alien baby was normal. And yet, it was just part of my daily life.

The discomfort I expected finally happened. My lower back ached constantly, no doubt due to my size. In the two weeks since Zat'tor pollinated me, my stomach had grown to astronomical proportions. It looked like someone had strapped an overblown beach ball to my middle. Jaeyoung spent a lot of time examining me, asking questions, and taking notes. He insisted on near-daily check-ups, but eventually I stopped thinking they were for my sake and instead realized they were an outlet for his curiosity.

"And you say there's no pain today?" he asked, scribbling notes down on some parchment Fhi'ran had given him.

"No," I said, bored. "Not today, not yesterday, or the day before…"

"And hopefully never," Zat'tor chimed in. He sat next to me with his arm looped around my shoulder. He accompanied me everywhere, so naturally, he came along to every doctor's visit.

"That would be nice, but I doubt it," I remarked.

"Why?"

"Because human births aren't painless unless there's drugs involved."

"And epidurals are in short supply on Eukaria," Jaeyoung said wryly. He brought over some kind of liquid concoction in a ceramic cup. "Drink this. Fhi'ran taught me it's full of vitamins for child bearers."

I wrinkled my nose at the sour scent. "Do I have to?"

Jaeyoung arched a brow. "Do you see a drug mart nearby where you can buy your prenatal vitamins? Drink it."

I sighed and tipped the cup back. To my surprise, it tasted more pleasant than it smelled.

"You must keep your strength up," Zat'tor murmured, nuzzling my head. "Whatever the healer says, you must do."

"Yeah, I will. So, have you figured out the mystery of my pregnancy yet?" I asked Jaeyoung.

He crossed his arms. "No. It's difficult to make progress without the tools I'd need at my disposal. And it's not like I can open you up to take a look."

Zat'tor growled and held me closer possessively.

"Relax," I said, patting his shoulder. "He just said he *wasn't* going to do that."

"But he thought about it," Zat'tor grumbled.

Jaeyoung shrugged, not offended by Zat'tor's bristling. "I'm a scientist at heart. I like to know things. But I'm also Levi's doctor. I wouldn't put him at risk like that."

"Perhaps you should gain first-hand experience by bearing your own baby," Zat'tor suggested.

I snorted, thinking it was a joke, but when he didn't laugh, I realized it wasn't. "Oh. You're serious."

Jaeyoung let out a scoff-laugh hybrid. "No, thank you. Like I said before, I'm not the romantic type."

Zat'tor made a face, like he knew something Jaeyoung didn't. I raised a brow but didn't pry. Whatever the future held, it would play out on its own.

"So, what exactly should I do?" I asked. "Like, what's going to happen when the baby finally wants to come out? My body's not exactly designed for this..."

Sensing my anxiety, Zat'tor frowned sympathetically at me. His hand found my knee and squeezed it gently. I linked my fingers with his. The monumental size difference between our hands was comforting, like Zat'tor's body was big and strong enough to smother my concerns.

Jaeyoung gave me a calm, even glance. "I'll be straight with you, Levi. I don't know what's going to happen. I have no experience or data to base my theory on. I've asked Fhi'ran and he doesn't know of any other species breeding with a Maeleon."

That wasn't the most reassuring reply in the world. I swallowed the lump in my throat.

"But that doesn't mean it will go poorly," Jaeyoung went on, offering me a small smile. "Your pregnancy has been going amazingly well. Far better than I expected, to be honest. I suspect it has less to do with your body's limitations and more with Maeleon biology."

His confident attitude eased my shaky nerves. "What do you mean?" I asked.

"I believe Zat'tor's pollen altered your physiology," Jaeyoung stated. "My theory is that it awakened a makeshift womb inside your body. Somehow, against all odds, it avoided rejection from your system. In layman's terms, it's possible the pollen copied your DNA and created a womb-like construct from it."

My head spun. This was so much information to take in. It sounded unbelievable, but Jaeyoung said it with a straight face. Could that all be true? We didn't have our high-tech Earth technology to scan my body and check. All I had was Jaeyoung's theory.

"Okay," I said, nodding slowly. "But what about the, uh... exit strategy?"

"I've been thinking about that, too," Jaeyoung stated. "Again, all I have are theories. I have no way of knowing until I see it for myself."

"Real helpful, Doc," I mumbled.

Jaeyoung smiled gently. "I'm not concerned, Levi. I doubt Zat'tor's pollen would go through all that effort of creating a womb without also prompting creation of a channel for the fetus to breach."

I wrinkled my nose at his unpleasant terminology. "So, what you're saying is, the baby's coming out one way or the other?"

"Plainly, yes."

"And that way might be... my butt."

"Anything is possible," Jaeyoung said.

I wasn't sure how I felt about that, but I had no choice. I

glanced at Zat'tor. "How are Maeleons usually born?" I asked.

Zat'tor curled his tentacle around my arm thoughtfully. "I have never witnessed a birth with my own eyes, but I hear it is a magical experience."

"That's even *less* helpful," I grumbled.

He smiled blissfully at me. It was hard to stay in a bad mood when he did that.

"Guess that's it, then," I said. "Any other weird pre-natal juices I should drink, or can I go now?"

Jaeyoung nodded. "You're all good for today, Levi. Get plenty of rest, light exercise if you're up for it, eat well, and drink water. There's nothing more we can do until it's time for the birth."

"Whenever that is," I murmured, glancing at my swollen, beach-ball body. It just seemed to get bigger and bigger.

Was it ever going to stop, or was I going to end up floating around as one of Eukaria's moons?

"You are too anxious, Levi," Zat'tor murmured in my ear after we left the den. "Let me take care of you."

I smiled, leaning into him. It had become a habit since we'd gotten together. His tall, broad frame comforted me, and I liked using him as my own personal support—both literally and emotionally.

"You already take care of me every second of every day," I commented.

"So, let me do it now."

Zat'tor didn't wait for my waffling response. He looped his tentacles around my midsection and chest, feeling me up in the middle of the village. I blushed and half-heartedly swatted them, even though I knew Maeleons had no qualms about PDA.

"Hey, c'mon, at least wait until we're back in the den," I said through a grin.

"I can barely contain myself," Zat'tor growled in my ear, sending a shiver down my spine. He buried the tip of his snout in my neck, sniffing it deeply. "Your body is irresistible."

A jolt of arousal ignited in my blood. I blew out a shaky breath. Zat'tor thought *I* was irresistible, and yet he did things like this to me, right in front of everybody. He gave me no choice but to react. Dirty alien perv.

I dragged him back to the den before we engaged in public indecency acts that would get us arrested back on Earth. As soon as we were in private, we crashed together. Zat'tor kissed me hard. He wrapped his arms around my lower back while his tentacles slipped beneath my armpits, holding me upright. I melted into his grasp and let him carry my weight.

I yelped as Zat'tor picked me up bridal-style. Even with my additional pregnancy weight, Zat'tor never faltered. Warmth filled me. I'd never felt as comfortable and safe as I did in his arms.

"Gorgeous," he growled in between kisses.

My heart fluttered as love and lust mingled below my belly. Intimacy with Zat'tor was indescribable. It felt dream-like, yet so painfully, wonderfully real. It was a feeling I knew I'd never experience back on Earth with any human man. Zat'tor was special.

He braced himself against the wall and sank down, all the while holding me in his arms so I didn't touch the floor.

His physical strength always stunned me. Was there anything he couldn't do?

Zat'tor paused as his gaze ran across my midsection. He stroked my swollen belly with gentle, sweeping motions. A purr vibrated in his chest.

"Never have you looked so gorgeous," Zat'tor murmured, causing me to shiver. "I will spend today worshipping you."

I blushed to the tips of my extremities. Hearing that never got old.

"Tell me what you desire," Zat'tor asked, his voice thick with lust.

"Everything. Anything," I breathed.

"You want me to fill you?"

"Yes, please."

He grinned, his sharp teeth gleaming in the dim atmospheric light of the den. Lifting me with his tentacles, he readied his cock. It slipped out of the hidden slit between his thighs, worming its way towards my twitching hole. My chest rose and fell rapidly as I breathed hard in anticipation.

The second the tip of his cock brushed against my entrance, I groaned. Even that small touch felt so fucking good. I must've been crazed with pregnancy hormones or something. I loved it.

I didn't need to warm up. My hole stretched, instantly accommodating Zat'tor's slick intrusion. His cock squirmed inside me, brushing against every ring of muscle and shooting electric jolts of pleasure up my spine. My brain turned to mush—every neuron was flooded with lust. All I knew was how fucking good Zat'tor made me feel.

"I will make you experience ultimate pleasure," Zat'tor promised in a throaty voice.

He held me hovering above his cock as he plowed in

and out in a steady rhythm. Drool trickled down my open, moaning mouth. I was delirious.

"Fuck," I managed to say. It was probably the only word I *could* say at the moment. Thinking was hard enough, but speaking was basically impossible. Every other sound that escaped my lips was a needy whimper or wanton moan, begging for more.

Zat'tor wasn't content to just fuck me, though. His large hands found my cock, straining against the bottom of my belly, and began stroking it. Hot pleasure erupted in my veins. I cried out, bucking into Zat'tor's grasp.

"Fuck, fuck, fuck," I whined. "That feels so fucking good…"

His cock inched deeper inside my ass, filling me absolutely. I hissed out through my teeth. I felt ready to pop in more ways than one, but it was a satisfying sensation.

"Kiss me," I begged.

Zat'tor angled his maw towards my mouth. Our tongues intertwined in a wet dance, shooting pleasure through my whole body. Every sensation felt heightened. I wasn't going to last.

Zat'tor must've felt it. He kissed me harder, fucked me deeper, jacked off my cock faster.

It all culminated in one big moment of ecstasy. I screamed, raw and loud, as fireworks of pleasure exploded across my every nerve. I came in thick jets across the backs of Zat'tor's hands. He continued to pump my sensitive cock until my throes ended. I heard him grunt as he came, too— and of course, I felt the flood of pollen filling my insides, stretching me to my very limit. The warmth of it made me shudder. Hell, it threatened to turn me on again.

But then, it happened.

I didn't know what *it* was, but I sure as hell felt it.

Still gasping for air, I paused. Zat'tor met my gaze.

"What is it?" he asked.

"I... don't know," I admitted. His cock was still inside me. Was that what I felt?

No, it wasn't quite the same. I recognized that by now. This was a different sensation.

"Uh," I said warily. "I think something's happening to me."

Zat'tor's eyes widened. "What is it? Are you hurt?"

I grimaced, shifting my body slightly to gauge it. There was no sharp pain, but there was discomfort, like an aching muscle.

"Maybe," I admitted.

"Let me release you," Zat'tor said urgently.

Careful but quick, Zat'tor retracted his spent cock. As the space opened up within my body, I gasped. There was still *something* there, and it wasn't my mate's erection.

The discomfort worsened into a pain like a cramp. It wasn't a pain I recognized. It was new, and therefore terrifying.

Then it suddenly dawned on me what was happening.

"Zat'tor," I said with a crack in my voice. "I think I'm about to give birth."

As SOON AS the words left Levi's mouth, my world stopped. My filum was birthing soon. His safety and the health of our baby were my first priorities.

"All right," I said, staying as calm as possible.

"I don't know what's happening," Levi whimpered, "but you're gonna stay with me, right?"

I squeezed his hand. "Always," I promised.

He bit his lip, gaze darting to the door. "What about the healers? I'm freaking out. I can't do this by myself."

"I will take you to them. We won't be separated."

Levi nodded slowly. He looked vulnerable and small. He must've been so scared. I held him close to my chest as I stood. I'd do anything in my power to ease his nerves.

"It will be all right," I promised, because I knew it would be.

Levi said nothing. Cold sweat broke out across his skin and he trembled like a falling leaf. It pained me to see him so afraid, but I understood why. There was no precedent for a human birthing a Maeleon's baby.

"Levi, look at me," I urged.

He blinked up with wide, wavering eyes.

"Everything will be fine," I said, soft but confident. "You, the baby, and me—the three of us have a bright future ahead of us. I know this to the depths of my bones. The unknown is scary, but I'm right here with you. You won't face it alone."

The tautness evaporated from Levi's frame. He let out a long, shaky breath and flashed a hesitant smile.

"It's weird how much I believe it when you say it," he said.

I pressed a chaste kiss to his forehead. He was warm and damp with sweat.

As I stormed into the healers' den, both Fhi'ran and Jaeyoung got to their feet. I didn't know if it was our hasty arrival or their healers' intuition, but they read the situation instantly.

"Is it happening?" Jaeyoung asked.

I spoke so Levi didn't have to push himself. "Levi suspects the baby is coming," I told them.

Fhi'ran gestured to a raised surface. "Come, place your filum here."

They'd prepared a comfortable bed for Levi in advance. Everyone in the village was looking forward to his birthing, but the healers took a keener interest than the rest. I laid Levi down, careful of his aching back. His brows were knitted in discomfort.

I stayed close, keeping my hands and tentacles on his arm. I needed to be in contact with him. I wouldn't let him suffer alone.

"Does it hurt?" Jaeyoung asked, taking his place by Levi's feet.

Levi's jaw tensed as he nodded.

"It's all right, Levi, you'll get through this. Let's start by spreading your legs," Jaeyoung instructed. "Deep breaths. In, out."

Levi did as he was told and focused on his breathing. "Phew... This is a lot. Ow."

Sweat prickled his skin, and his hands curled into fists. It was the most I'd heard him complain since his pregnancy began. I wished I could do more to ease his pain...

An idea came to me. Maybe there *was* something I could do.

My feelers slowly floated towards him. The tips hovered above Levi's chest. He noticed them, panting hard, then met my gaze and nodded.

Accepting Levi's invitation, I allowed the tips of my tendrils to burrow into his chest. The second they breached his skin, they turned ethereal, like morning mist. Levi gasped and shuddered at the feeling, but it didn't add to his discomfort. I knew because I felt exactly what he felt. The deep, aching pain was interspersed with sharp jolts of agony that came and went in waves. I ground my teeth as the pain washed over me, too. My poor, sweet filum.

"Are all human births like this?" I asked roughly.

"You mean painful? If so, then yes, generally speaking," Jaeyoung answered. "But on Earth, we have ways to dull the pain."

"Zat'tor, wait," Levi said, putting his hands on my feelers. His palms were clammy with sweat. "I don't want you to suffer."

He was too kind. I placed my hand on his.

"You did not know this would happen when I pollinated you," I reminded him. "It's my responsibility to bear this burden alongside you. I will be fine."

Levi made a sad face, but he must've realized I wouldn't agree, so he saved his breath.

"Here, Levi," Fhi'ran said, offering him a drink. "This will help the pain."

Levi smiled gratefully and sipped from the cup. "Hey, this tastes better than the stuff you gave me before."

He sounded relieved, like he was already in less agony. I felt the change in his system. As I weathered the pain alongside him, his share lightened.

"Good," Jaeyoung said. "Keep breathing like that. Steady."

"What's even going on down there?" Levi grumbled. He sounded more annoyed than agonized, which was good. Our assistance was working.

Jaeyoung didn't respond. He stared at Levi's body, blinking in thought.

"Hello?" Levi called when he didn't reply.

"Sorry," Jaeyoung said. "I've never seen anything like this before."

"Great. Really reassuring, Doc..."

"It's not bad," Jaeyoung corrected. "I'm intrigued. How do you feel?"

"Okay, I guess," Levi said. He smiled in my direction. "Zat'tor's helping."

Jaeyoung glanced at where my feelers touched Levi's chest, but turned his focus back to Levi's body. He seemed fascinated. I was intrigued by his curiosity, so I leaned towards him to see what he saw.

I immediately understood. Levi's hole—the one I'd stretched earlier today—was open. Something pink and gold and fleshy emerged from it.

"Fhi'ran, do you recognize this?" Jaeyoung asked his fellow healer.

"Ah, yes," Fhi'ran confirmed. "That is the birthing chamber from which all Maeleons are born."

Levi sat halfway upright. "What? Birthing chamber? What're you talking about? I can't see!"

The jolt of his anxiety and excitement came through my feelers. I sent a pulse of tranquil energy through them, hoping to calm him. When he felt it, he sighed in relief and loosened his shoulders.

"Thanks, Zat'tor," he said softly. "That feels good. But seriously, what's going on?"

"My suspicions were right," Jaeyoung said. "Just as it created a womb with your DNA, Zat'tor's pollen also created a natural exit for the baby."

Levi tilted his head. "Let me guess. It's coming out of my butt?"

"It's coming out of a fleshy tube that's coming out of your butt," Jaeyoung corrected.

Levi snorted in amusement. "Nobody on Earth would *ever* believe this..."

"That's why we live on Eukaria now," Jaeyoung said wryly. "How's your pain level?"

A tired smile curved across Levi's lips. "It's fine with the weird juice Fhi'ran gave me and with Zat'tor's help."

"Good, because the channel is pulsating."

Levi frowned. "What does that mean?"

Jaeyoung shot a glance between his legs. "The baby's coming out. Right now."

A pulse of Levi's panic came through the feelers, but I counteracted it with a wave of calm. He exhaled a shaky breath.

"Okay," he murmured. "I can do this. Right? Someone please tell me I can do this."

"You can do it, Levi," I told him. "You've done excellently thus far."

He nodded and sank back into the bed. "Tell me what to do, Doc."

"The channel seems to be doing most of the work for you," Jaeyoung remarked. "It's pushing the baby out towards us. All you need to do is help it along."

Curiosity got the best of me. I leaned over to witness the birth. The channel that had emerged from Levi stretched and undulated as a form moved inside of it.

A burst of happiness bloomed in my chest. That was our baby!

Levi gasped, sounding lighter. My feelers were still connected with him, so he felt my unbridled joy, too. It gave him the strength to push hard one final time. With a great big heave, a slimy form emerged from the end of the channel. My heart raced. That curled-up lump nestled on the bed was our newborn.

"What happened?" Levi asked between short breaths.

The room was silent with awe. Even the cool-headed Jaeyoung was speechless at the sight of the baby, his dark eyes shining with emotion.

I moved first. I reached for the newborn, picking it up gently. Our baby squirmed inside the translucent gold sac. Instinct awakened inside me. I cut a hole in the sac with my claw, allowing the newborn to spill out of it.

"Is that our baby?" Levi asked breathlessly, his voice wavering.

He sat upright and reached out with his arms in a silent plea. As I placed our infant in his lap, a huge smile broke across his face and tears formed in the corners of his eyes. He was absolutely elated.

The newborn was a Maeleon, there was no doubt about that. Its body was the same color as a healthy new leaf. But when the infant opened its eyes and blinked, I noticed oddly human irises—the same shade of green as Levi's.

"Hi there," Levi murmured, beaming. "You're so beautiful, aren't you?"

My heart felt so full. My human filum had given birth to a Maeleon, but there was no hesitation to Levi's love. It was unconditional. That was his baby, no matter the shape or species.

Jaeyoung and Fhi'ran came closer to see the newborn.

"Congratulations, you two," Jaeyoung said with the brightest smile I'd ever seen. "I'm no expert, but that looks like one happy, healthy infant."

"Not an expert *yet*," Fhi'ran commented. "You've been a wonderful help in the healer's den."

Jaeyoung looked pleased at the praise. "Thank you. I hope to continue learning for a long time." He turned back to Levi and the squirming newborn. "Have you thought of a name?"

Levi laughed softly and caught my gaze. "It all happened so fast... There wasn't really time. We never talked about it, did we?"

I shook my head. "Maeleons wait until their young are born to gift names. What would *you* like to name our baby, Levi?"

"I had a few ideas bouncing around. They were all kinda gender-specific, but I guess Maeleons don't think that way, huh?" He grinned at the baby, who looked around the room curiously with big green eyes. "I want a name that reflects both human and Maeleon culture."

"Tell me your ideas," I asked.

"I was thinking of naming the baby after my mother, Daisy." Levi smiled at the newborn. "So, if we said it the Maeleon way, her name would be Dai'zee."

My chest filled with warmth. "That's beautiful." I mulled over the new word, *her*. "You will teach me how to use these 'pronouns' correctly, yes?"

"Of course," Levi replied.

"Dai'zee," I echoed, glancing at our newborn.

As if responding to her own name, Dai'zee turned her green-eyed gaze to me. I shivered. Her eyes looked so much like Levi's that it stunned me. We shared a long, meaningful stare until Dai'zee parted her jaws and squeaked loudly.

"Dai'zee must be hungry," Fhi'ran remarked.

"Crap. She needs to eat. What do baby Maeleons eat?" Levi demanded.

I chuckled, putting my tentacle around his shoulders reassuringly. "Their teeth are not yet formed, so they can't eat."

"What?"

"Come outside with Dai'zee. You'll see," I promised.

I steadied Levi with my tentacles, helping him stand up and walk outside the den. The sun shone bright in the sky, as if welcoming Dai'zee's arrival. I basked in its warming rays with a silent smile of gratitude.

After cleaning up and slipping into his onesie, Levi stepped out into the sun with a squirming Dai'zee in his arms. Immediately, the newborn relaxed. She yawned and stretched out her tiny feelers and tentacles, raising them into the light.

"Whoa," Levi murmured, eyes widening at the display. "I just remembered you telling me a long time ago that Maeleons photosynthesize. I kinda thought you were joking. But look at her. She's like a little flower."

Jaeyoung came out behind us. He scribbled notes on his clipboard. "How fascinating."

"She'll bask like this until her teeth come in," I told them. "After that, she can also eat solid food."

Levi nodded, relieved that his baby wouldn't go hungry. He pressed Dai'zee closer to his chest in an adorable embrace as she basked.

"I'm happy everything went well today," he said with a contented sigh.

"I told you it would," I reminded him.

"True. I should've just believed my filum, huh?" Levi teased.

Hearing him embrace that term meant so much to me. I smiled, looping my arm around his upper back.

"I love you, Levi," I said.

My filum's expression lit up. The sunlight reflected off his eyes, casting glints of gold in the green. "I love you, Zat'tor."

I leaned down, bridging the space between us as I placed a kiss on his soft lips.

A loud gasp interrupted our kiss. I hadn't noticed until now, but a loose crowd had formed around the healer's den —no doubt everyone waiting excitedly for Levi's delivery. A familiar human face emerged and rushed towards us.

"Is that the baby?" Paz blurted, a huge grin splitting his cheeks. He raced over without waiting for an answer. "Levi, you did it! You gave birth to a real-life baby!"

Levi gave him a flustered smile. "Yeah, I guess I did."

Jaeyoung looked both amused and deeply proud of his friend. "Congratulations. Not only did you successfully deliver a newborn, you are officially the first cis man to ever do so."

"Do I win a trophy?" Levi asked.

"Your *baby* is the trophy, obviously," Paz said. He looked overjoyed as he brought his face closer to Dai'zee.

"Who's the cutest little Maeleon? You are." He pouted. "Aww, I kinda want one too. Don't you?"

"No," Jaeyoung said, deadpan.

"I don't believe that for a second," Paz shot back without hesitation. He pressed his cheek next to Dai'zee's. "How can you resist this face?"

Dai'zee turned her head and gummed Paz's cheek, making him giggle. I did not think he was being hyperbolic. Now that he knew it was possible, I could practically feel Paz's desire for a Maeleon baby of his own forming in real time. But there was no rush. Only time would tell when his turn would come.

"Phew," Levi said, leaning against me. "Dai'zee has the right idea. I'm starving."

"You worked very hard," I reminded him. "Let's get some food in you."

Levi grinned eagerly. "How does that manage to sound both sweet *and* sexy when you say it?"

SOMETHING INTERESTING HAPPENED to me the day after Dai'zee's birth.

Our little family spent the morning outside, basking together for our daughter's meal. Zat'tor and Dai'zee closed their eyes, letting their feelers float towards the sky like wispy outstretched arms. The whole photosynthesis thing was a surprise, but considering how closely Maeleons resembled plants, it made sense. Since I couldn't turn the sun into nutrients like my mate and daughter, I just enjoyed the sun the old-fashioned human way.

I released a contented sigh as we sat outside together in the grass, letting the sun soak into our skin. A cool breeze flowed through the village, ruffling my hair.

At first, it sounded like a whisper. I chalked it up to the sound of the wind.

But then the whispering grew louder, and the formless breeze warped into something that sounded like a recogniz-able word.

My eyes snapped open. I looked around to see if Zat'tor

had said anything, but he was silent and tranquil. No other villagers were around. There was nobody who could've spoken.

Brushing it off as my imagination, I closed my eyes again and relaxed.

The whisper came again. It was soft, a delicate murmur close to my ear. A shiver jolted me. It felt like a voice was calling out to me in words I couldn't make sense of, yet still understood.

I slowly rose to my feet. The motion pulled Zat'tor from his trance. Dai'zee was still dozing in his lap.

"Is everything all right, Levi?" he asked.

"Yeah," I said distantly. "I hear... something."

Zat'tor's gaze flashed. "Ah. It finally happened."

"Huh?"

He stood beside me, cradling Dai'zee in his strong arms. A knowing expression lit up his eyes. "Come. Let's go to the Sweetfields."

I followed silently, distracted by the whispering in my head. My heart picked up speed as we reached the edge of the sprawling flower fields. The voices were louder here. Each word was crystal clear, like it was being spoken against the rim of my ear. I couldn't translate the words into human language. The translation module didn't modify it, either—it bypassed the ITM and went directly into my brain.

"I hear them," I murmured.

Zat'tor smiled at me. "Didn't I promise you would eventually understand?"

I thought back to one of our earlier conversations, back when we cleaned up the ship's wreckage. Zat'tor said he heard the voices of the flowers. I'd assumed he was being figurative—until now.

I closed my eyes and breathed in the fresh, sweet air.

Floral scents danced around us as the breeze carried the aroma across the land. The flower voices weren't overwhelming or overly loud. They were comforting. Welcoming. As soon as I recognized them, they blended pleasantly into the background like a gossamer song.

"I get it now," I said softly, my voice blending into one of thousands. "Can you hear them?"

"Always," Zat'tor replied.

"Can Dai'zee hear them, too?"

"Yes. And I am sure in time, Paz and Jaeyoung will hear them, too."

Zat'tor was convinced that my friends would find Maeleon mates the same way I did. I'd brushed it off as him being a romantic sap at first, but now I wasn't so sure. Jaeyoung was already deeply invested in Maeleon culture. He spent most of his time learning the local healing arts, and Linn'ar spent most of *his* time not-so-subtly poking around the healer's den. Paz, too, kept fidgeting near the edge of the village, as if looking forward to a specific person's return. He reminded me of a dog waiting for its owner to come back home. I hoped for his sake that whoever it was hurried up.

Dai'zee yawned with a squeak. Her teeth were already starting to come out. I chuckled at the sight of them.

"What is it?" Zat'tor asked.

"I just remembered when we first landed here and I was terrified of your sharp teeth," I said with a grin. "That feels like an entire lifetime ago."

Zat'tor's expression was warm. "Yes, it does. My life felt like it could not begin until I met you."

The statement unleashed butterflies in my chest. I laughed, throwing myself into Zat'tor's embrace. His multiple limbs always came in handy; he could carry our daughter in his arms while also hugging me with his tentacles.

I'd take my sexy alien partner over a boring old human any day.

THE END

Printed in Great Britain
by Amazon

29282110R00101